CITY OF SMOKE AND SEA

a novel

. . .

Malia Márquez

 Red Hen Press | *Pasadena,*

City of Smoke and Sea
Copyright © 2025 by Malia Márquez
All Rights Reserved

No part of this book may be used or reproduced in any manner whatsoever without the prior written permission of both the publisher and the copyright owner.

Book design by Mark E. Cull

Library of Congress Cataloging-in-Publication Data

Names: Márquez, Malia, author.
Title: City of smoke and sea / a novel Malia Márquez.
Description: First edition. | Pasadena, CA: Red Hen Press, 2025.
Identifiers: LCCN 2024024538 (print) | LCCN 2024024539 (ebook) | ISBN 9780963952837 (paperback) | ISBN 9780963952899 (ebook)
Subjects: LCGFT: Thrillers (Fiction) | Detective and mystery fiction. | Novels.
Classification: LCC PS3613.A76774 C58 2025 (print) | LCC PS3613.A76774 (ebook) | DDC 813/.6—dc23/eng/20240604
LC record available at https://lccn.loc.gov/2024024538
LC ebook record available at https://lccn.loc.gov/2024024539

The National Endowment for the Arts, the Los Angeles County Arts Commission, the Ahmanson Foundation, the Dwight Stuart Youth Fund, the Max Factor Family Foundation, the Pasadena Tournament of Roses Foundation, the Pasadena Arts & Culture Commission and the City of Pasadena Cultural Affairs Division, the City of Los Angeles Department of Cultural Affairs, the Audrey & Sydney Irmas Charitable Foundation, the Meta & George Rosenberg Foundation, the Albert and Elaine Borchard Foundation, the Adams Family Foundation, the Riordan Foundation, Amazon Literary Partnership, the Sam Francis Foundation, and the Mara W. Breech Foundation partially support Red Hen Press.

First Edition
Published by Red Hen Press
Pasadena, CA
www.redhen.org

For E, C & L

Black Sheep's destinies are not in
necessarily having families,
having prescribed existences—like the American Dream.
Black Sheep destinies are to give
meaning in life—to be angels,
to be conscience, to be nightmares
to be actors in dreams.

—Karen Finlay

In the first place, we don't like to be called "refugees."

—Hannah Arendt

One

The sky over the Pacific was whale gray the day I went for an interview at Vista Mar. It matched my mood and my outlook. At an early stage of my recovery following the accident, a counselor told me it's impossible to go from unhappy to happy, she said you've got to find some neutral territory between the two in order to make the transition. At the time, I imagined it in terms of colors, of saturation. The washed-out gray green of a hospital wall compared to the green buds of a tree in spring. Both green, but definitely not the same. For a long time, I didn't even try. Now, I was trying, but I still felt pretty washed out, overcast like the sky.

The past several years had been pretty crap. There was dropping out of college and returning home to my grandma's house in Los Angeles, years of restaurant work when what I really wanted was a writing career, and my terrible on-again, off-again boyfriend, Arlo—currently my ex but whom I still hadn't entirely managed to extract myself from. Then the car accident . . . which I'd survived. The tinge of hope I'd been feeling recently was likely related to this second chance I'd been given, to my full recovery from the accident and all that preceded it, a mess which, if I were being honest with myself, was all Arlo-adjacent. My healing I credited to Gran, to the love and care she'd poured into me while I was in the hospital. She also got me this job interview. The owner, Wyatt Jones, was an old friend of hers. And while I did slightly dread the prospect of yet another dead-end serving position in a restaurant in my hometown, I was grateful for the opportunity. I needed money and I needed to get on with my life.

I'd heard Vista Mar was upscale, that I could make a fortune in tips. A fortune according to my own modest standards, of course. Slamming my car door shut, I paused a moment to look out, past black asphalt parking lot, green dumpsters along a scuffed stucco wall, to the wind-capped surf rolling into shore.

I hoped I wouldn't let Gran down by letting my melancholy mess this up. Nobody wants a glum waitress, least of all me. I supposed I was grateful the sun wasn't out to shine a light on what was still missing in me, what had not yet healed. Perhaps this place, Vista Mar, would be my neutral territory. I drew in a deep breath of salt air, hot grease, and fried things from what must be the kitchen exhaust fan, and the special vinegar stench of food waste trapped in garbage bags all nestled together in those dumpsters. It was all familiar, but this time I was determined to do things differently. I walked around the building to the front door, a heavy wooden Art Deco–style monstrosity that may actually have held on since the 1930s, and entered.

The restaurant itself was classic, opened as an exclusive beach club in the thirties and converted to an upscale seafood bistro sometime in the sixties. Over a long, polished wood bar hung a huge framed painting of a lounging tiger, teeth bared on black velvet, crouched over rows of glistening, backlit bottles of liquor. A tall man with brown skin that glowed from the inside, several shades darker than mine, nodded to me as I entered, not pausing his rhythm of polishing glasses with a frayed white towel. A steady wind off the ocean cut through the restaurant, whooshing over dark wood tables already set with cutlery, small square side plates, and cloudy green bottles of olive oil. Through paned glass windows could be seen metallic-gray water and sky like two sides of a cooking pot, ornamented by curling wisps of cloud and surf. The salt air mingled with steamy garlic and lemon emanating from the swing doors at the other end of the bar, and the slightly raunchy seaweed scent of low tide. Goosebumps prickled my forearms. It seemed this was a place where *things happened*. Whether it was the brisk air, Billie Holiday loud on the sound system making everything sexy and hyper-real, or the striking bartender, I had the irrational sensation I'd escaped my mundane existence— was perhaps on the verge of breaking my going-nowhere pattern.

"Queenie Rivers?" said a voice from behind me. Startled, I turned, blinking as my eyes adjusted to the contrast of muted yellow light from lamps illuminating the windowless entry and the natural light filling the dining room beyond. A lean blond woman, likely a few years younger than me, stood at the host station, pen poised over a notebook. She wore a navy blazer and had a hungry look in her eyes—the aspiring actress type who eventually finds a successful career as a fitness instructor or real estate agent. I'd overcompensated for my nervousness by marching in, right past the old-fashioned cloakroom and host station to where the bar looked out on the restaurant, and beyond a wall of windows and wide-open glass patio doors, the sea.

"Yes, hi!" I tucked my wavy hair behind my ears and tugged at the hem of my black skirt, painfully aware that I'd bought it in a secondhand shop I don't even remember when. This was my first job interview since the accident.

Truth was, I didn't want to be there, didn't want the job. But I needed it, and Gran had made the effort to get me the opportunity.

She looked me up and down, the expression on her narrow, foxlike face nonplussed. "Mr. Jones will see you in his office," she said, and crossed something on the page out with her pen. Presumably, me.

"Okay," I said. I stood there, waiting for her to show me the way, but she made no move, just kept scribbling in that notebook and looking put together as hell. I bet money she wears cashmere sweater sets, I thought. Or if she doesn't now, she will one day. I coughed to get her attention, thinking maybe she was so caught up in her scheduling or whatever she'd forgotten about me.

"Yes?" She raised her head, gazing somewhere beyond my left ear.

"Where's the office?"

With the pen, she pointed to a door to her right I hadn't noticed. "Upstairs," she said, as if I should have known. "Can't miss it."

"Oh, stop giving her a hard time, Rita. She doesn't even work here yet." The bartender spoke while holding a wine glass by the stem up to the natural light that poured from the many windows that looked out on the Pacific. Though he looked to be about forty-five, his voice carried the gravity of a much older person. "Be nice," he said, narrowing his eyes at her.

The woman smiled, or rather, appeared to try to smile, but it didn't reach her eyes. She cleared her throat with a delicate cough and shook her hair back from her face. "I'm Rita, the hostess here at Vista Mar." She paused, cocked her head to examine me. "That's Pirate, the bartender and our resident knight in shining armor." I shook the chilly manicured hand Rita offered, which she pulled back quickly as if I'd shocked her. "Does that pass muster?" she asked Pirate, then let out a startling peal of laughter that made me jump. The bartender rolled his eyes.

"Nice to meet you, Rita. And . . . Pirate," I breathed, nodding to the bartender.

He chuckled. "She's just messing with you," he said, holding a pint glass up to inspect it for smudges. "Does it to everyone. Can't take it personally."

"There's one door at the top of the stairs. That's Wyatt Jones's office," Rita said, waving me back to a door by the cloakroom, making a show of opening it for me. "Wyatt and Shen are in a meeting, but he knows you're coming."

"Thanks," I said, hitching my leather bag up on my shoulder. I brushed past her as I stepped around the station to the door, sensed rather than saw her shrink back from the physical contact. Good. If I got the job, I could tell Rita would be my greatest obstacle. Best to establish myself as no pushover right off the bat. The stairs were carpeted in faded forest green with gold fleur-de-lis. Wood-paneled walls, the nice old kind, were illuminated by glass sconces leading to a landing at the top and a miniature of the main door. Brushed glass panels in the top half promised light on the other side. The air went still when the door clicked shut behind me. As I took the narrow steps two at a time, holding my breath like I do when I'm anxious, I was thinking the building must have squatted there by the ocean quite a long time and been well taken care of to have all these perfectly preserved historical details.

At the top I let out my breath, blood rushing loudly in my ears in the confined space. I knocked. No answer, but I could hear muffled voices within. I knocked again, louder. Hot from taking the stairs so quickly and beginning to feel claustrophobic, I reached for the knob.

The first thing I noticed was a Russian doll on the shelf that looked just like the one at home, on our kitchen shelf, where Gran kept her petty cash, a matryoshka—an odd coincidence. The second thing was a fog of cigarette smoke. The third: two men by a large desk, partially obscured by the haze. I coughed as smoke snaked over on the draft from opening the door directly into my throat. One guy had his back to me, leaning on the desk facing the other one. He must have heard the door creak open and turned, shoulder-length shiny black hair framing features contorted into an expression of extreme upset, whether at my entrance or the conversation, I couldn't tell.

The other man, who I assumed was Wyatt because he conveyed extreme boss energy, reclined in a chair behind the desk smoking a cigarette. He had cropped silver hair, a strong chiseled jaw, and almond-shaped eyes. They were blue, bright blue like the sky on a clear July day. He appraised me like he already knew all about me, which maybe he did. Gran probably called to fill him in, though she hadn't said as much. Likely, this was a pity interview. Perhaps he'd already decided to give me the job as a favor to Gran.

Gran was a young eighty-four, but this man looked thirty years younger. How did they know each other again? He appeared healthy in spite of his smoking habit, though a little thickset around the middle, sun-kissed like most of us in SoCal.

"Well, hello," Wyatt said, breaking the silence. He stubbed out his cigarette in an overflowing brass ashtray. I watched the stream of white smoke thin and die, dispersing into invisible particles that touched everything in the room, including me. *Billie Holiday*, I reminded myself. *A sea view.*

"So, you're Queenie," Wyatt interrupted my thoughts. "Hmm, Anke Weiss's granddaughter." He shook his head in amazement.

"Anke Rivers, actually."

"Right! She married Cedric Rivers—soldier, right?"

"Officer," I corrected. "Grandad passed away several years ago."

"Oh, I'm sorry to hear it," Wyatt said sincerely. Seeming to sense I wanted to change the subject, he clapped his hands together. "Well, I spoke to your grandmother briefly. She said you have a lot of experience."

"Yes," I said. "I'm here to interview. You need waitstaff?"

"We do," Wyatt said. "Busy time of year and we just lost someone." Shen blinked at me. *Lost someone.* Like, they quit, or . . . ? The boss turned to Shen, clasped his upper arm, and said, "Don't worry, we'll figure it out."

"Sure thing, Wyatt," said Shen. His eyes shifted to me, and he pressed his lips together. Whatever he wanted to say, he wasn't going to say it in front of me.

"Please stop fretting, Shen, it never fixed anything," said Wyatt.

"I'm just concerned that if we don't act now—" He shot Wyatt a significant look.

"We need more information. Until then . . . keep digging," Wyatt said. Shen nodded, shook his head, nodded at me, and left. His footsteps rapidly descended the stairs. The door at the bottom slammed.

Wyatt walked over to a round window facing the ocean and cranked it open. Clear air flowed in, ruffling papers on the desk. "Shen's a worrier," he said, shaking his head. He returned to his chair and leaned back. "It's what makes him such a good accountant."

"Mm-hmm," I said, worrying about if I should stay standing in the middle of the room.

"What makes you good at your job?" Wyatt Jones asked, returning to his seat. I must have looked at him strangely because he smiled as if to put me at ease. "Please," he said, gesturing to a straight-backed chair positioned across from him at the desk, "sit." I wondered, idly, what type of information Shen was meant to be digging for, and whether I'd imagined the look of pity he'd shot me on his way out.

I sat, placing my bag on the floor beside my chair. I felt like a kindergartner about to be lectured. "Well, I don't currently have a job," I said, drumming up some artificial confidence. I crossed one leg over the other, sat up straight, and returned his easy, patronizing grin as best I could. "That's why I'm here."

Two

The day I was released from the hospital, Gran told me her version of what had happened the day of the accident. Having just returned from the brink of death (I saw the light, I wanted to enter it, but like most things, I just couldn't commit), I listened with interest.

Arlo had been driving his old jeep while I rode shotgun. We must have rounded the curve of the hill on Lincoln too fast, failed to slow with the yellow light, and shot through the intersection. Gran didn't describe the sound of screeching brakes, the smell of rubber on hot pavement, or the rain-like tinkling of shattering glass, but I can imagine it—or, perhaps, remember it.

When I think of it now, I imagine the watchers: the family about to cross to the bus stop at the light, grackles fussing over the picnic tables by the playground, other people in other cars as we careened into an unfortunately composed triquetra—three cars worth of deployed airbags and twisted metal. I have no idea if these imaginings (memories?) have any truth to them, but one wants to fill blank voids with something.

The driver of the blue sedan is frazzled, uninjured. The driver of the car with the smashed headlight waits for the airbag to deflate before gingerly pushing open the door. The driver of the jeep is still high on the lines he'd snorted from the dash before getting on the road. He's on his way to a lunch meeting with a couple of television executives he recently pitched an idea for a show. Now he will be late, which equals major points against him. He was already stressed about dropping his girlfriend off for her shift at a bistro in Culver City. His neck doesn't feel so good. He grits his teeth, pushing the airbag away from his face, barely noticing the minor cuts on his right hand and arm from the windshield glass, and looks over at the passenger seat. His girlfriend, Queenie Rivers (that's me), is slumped against the passenger door frame. Blood pours from the right side of her face, her neck, her shoulder . . . He can't tell where it's all coming from. Her window is shattered, from what he can see because her head slammed against it. Her eyes are closed.

Anke Weiss Rivers, my grandmother, sat in a cushioned armchair by my hospital bed every day for almost three weeks. When Arlo came to visit, she forgot his name. To be clear, she knew his name, but willfully forgot it for the purposes of the moment. You know how it goes. I was tucked deep inside a morphine-induced sleep at the time. I was alive, stable, breathing on my own since the doctors had somehow miraculously un-collapsed my lung. He entered looking part raccoon with his dark circled eyes and shifty, resourceful manner. He spoke quietly to me for a long time, or so Gran said.

I mention it to you now, Queenie, because it made me nervous. Whether he was whispering sweet nothings into your ear or blaming you for the opportunity he lost that day . . . He said they canned his project when he didn't show for a lunch meeting the day of the accident—his words, not mine. He's a coarse boy, Queenie. I don't know what you ever saw in him.

Maybe he whispered sweet nothings. Maybe he called me a con artist, or some other horribly offensive comment couched in humor. Had I been conscious (should these imagined exchanges have occurred), I would have returned the compliment by calling Arlo a baboon, an inside joke from our first date back in college when we visited the zoo in Central Park. Yes, I went to college in New York City, briefly. It didn't last long. When Arlo graduated and I essentially flunked out, we moved back to LA. A large male baboon had lumbered over to us, the only visitors, and pressed his inflamed ass to the plexiglass inches from our faces. I have nothing against baboons. Or maybe I do. See, the action felt violative, which encapsulates perfectly how I've often felt about Arlo and his behavior. Toxic masculinity baboonified, if you will. So, those words held secret power for me. They were a way to get inside Arlo's head, make him laugh. Make him recall a specific image and moment in time. But what he didn't understand was that I actually saw him that way sometimes, when he was being extra-specially an asshole. When I said those words, his face *was* the baboon butt pressed against the glass, which was something he could never take away from me.

Long before hospital visiting hours were over, Arlo rose, said goodbye to Gran, and left. She leaned forward to whisper in my ear. *Don't believe a word he says.* Once I was more alert, able to carry on a two-sided conversation, she kept saying it. And repeating it. And other helpful grandma tips too. So that by the time I was released into her care, not only had my body healed, but I had also transformed into an entirely other person. A person who would not go on a four-day coke bender and wake up under a pier. Who would not lose another waitressing job (or any job) for showing up hungover or not showing up at all. Who would not steal from her own grandparents, or the neighbors. Who would not endanger the lives of others by driving under the influence or with someone like Arlo, who was always under the influence.

A person who cared about her future.

A person who knew that when Arlo was speaking, I was chasing each of his seemingly innocuous little words with a handful of salt.

Sometimes I think it must have been divine, that light I saw. Or maybe my recovery was thanks to Gran focusing a steady beam of TLC on me for so many consecutive days while I was unable to wriggle out from under her laser-like love. Whatever the source of my grace, I emerged from the hospital like a butterfly from its chrysalis, my faith in the American Dream kindled, perhaps, for the first time in my life. I was ready to do things. Important things. I was going to spend my free time writing, finish that essay collection I began in college. I was going to get my own apartment near Gran's house and get a community garden plot. And compost. And participate in regular beach cleanups. Imagine my dismay as it began to sink in that none of those things were going to happen any time soon, that I was pretty much right where I started. I needed a job and the only job I was really qualified for was waiting tables.

It was Gran who suggested I apply at Vista Mar once I'd fully recovered. "Just give it a chance," she coaxed, pushing a plate of buttered toast, a mug of hot black coffee, and a newspaper toward me across the kitchen counter. She had circled the classifieds ad in blue pen. *Serving positions available at Vista Mar*, and a phone number to call. "I know the owner, Wyatt Jones. He's . . . very successful. You'd make decent money."

"You know that guy?" I'd heard of Wyatt Jones. And not all good. "How?"

"We worked together once, when I was younger," she answered vaguely. "You need your own place, Queenie," Gran sighed. "You need to live your own life."

"I need to get back to writing," I countered, accepting the toast. I leaned over to kiss Gran's powder-soft cheek. "But I'm tired. I can't seem to get anything underway, with recovering from the accident and all those bridges I burned with my old jobs . . ."

"You have no confidence," Gran said. There was no malice in her tone. It was a statement of fact.

"Yeah, but . . ."

"I'm glad you're clean, but your head's still all mixed up." She sliced a grapefruit, put one half in a bowl for herself and cut the rest into pieces for me. "I baby you."

"I love that you baby me." For the record, Gran never babied me.

"I know you do," she said. "That doesn't mean I'm helping you by doing it."

"I love you, Gran."

"And you know I love you. Why don't you find a program to finish your degree? Maybe then you can move on from . . ."

"I know, Gran," I said, biting into my toast, "I know."

As you know, I got the job. Sometimes, attainment feels like a curse. I didn't want to be a waitress, but for better or worse, that was what I was.

Three

On the way home from the interview at Vista Mar, my phone pinged, alerting me to a new text. Unable to resist, I glanced down at it. Just then, my aging Volkswagen convertible passed over a hunk of something in the road. There was a hollow, metallic thunk and I felt the impact as whatever it was collided with the undercarriage. A rattling sound, indicating some sort of damage I couldn't afford to fix, filled the car. I swore and smacked both hands on the wheel. If I hadn't been looking at my phone I might have avoided it. *If damn Arlo hadn't texted.* I rolled down all the windows in an attempt to drown out the racket. The content of the message only made matters worse because he was writing to share his latest victory with me; he'd sold a script to a producer whose work he "really digs."

Ugh. On so many levels.

I turned up the radio and drove, hoping the muffler wouldn't fall off. At the end of Gran's street, I turned into the parking lot of the local gas station for a soda. As Mrs. Lal, the proprietor, rang me up, she asked after Gran, of course. When I told her she was well and that she helped me get a job at Vista Mar, Mrs. Lal shook her head. "Watch out for that Wyatt Jones character," she said. "I hear he'll do anything for money." So the restaurant's shady reputation was more widespread than I knew. Then she asked if I was going with Gran to the next planning board meeting about the development of the nearby wetlands, because she and Mr. Lal would be there to fight against it. I said I probably wasn't because I would probably have to work. But Gran, as the main spokesperson for the conservation effort, would appreciate their support. Feeling awkward, I thanked her and hurried out, forgetting my ice-cold Dr Pepper, leaving it sweating there on Mrs. Lal's glass countertop.

Gran Rivers lived in a one-story bungalow on a winding street in the Del Rey Hills. Her house didn't exactly overlook the ocean, but you could feel it close by. My car groaned up the steeply sloped driveway, finally grating to a shuddering stop. As upset as I was, it was a relief to kill the engine. The shell-pink house was bathed in the golden afternoon light of late spring. I slumped back into my seat. "I got the job, Gran," I said to my reflection in the rearview mirror, which looked crushed. I would have to do better with the smile when I told her.

She must have been looking out the kitchen window because she flung wide the kitchen door before I even reached the stoop. At eighty-four, her back was straight as an arrow. Her chin-length bob had gone completely silver sometime before I'd been born. Her bone structure, visible beneath her glowing light brown skin, was strong and exact, like her. Her deep brown eyes flecked with gold appraised me from a distance. The deep-set, expressive lines of her face were arranged in such a way I could tell she was eager to know how the interview went. Eager for news of Wyatt Jones? She met me halfway down the drive, and, seeming to sense something was off, folded me into a hug without saying a word. Taking it in stride that her embrace made me start sobbing, she held me for a long time. I felt safe enveloped in her arms; her smell, a mix of cooking and the rose and sandalwood scent she always wore.

Gran led me into the house through the kitchen door to the sitting room and sat me down on the seafoam green velveteen sofa. Sun shone in the picture window that looked out on the street. A chrome bar cart with a crystal decanter half-filled with amber scotch caught the light. If I sat at the right angle, I found I could make it flash painfully but satisfyingly across my eyes. Nobody used the thing anymore. It hadn't been touched in the fifteen years since Grandad passed away. Gran preferred red wine. She said it kept her young. Perching on the ottoman across from me, she took a clean, pressed muslin handkerchief from her apron pocket and leaned forward to dab smudges from under my eyes.

"You look so tired . . . What is it, sweetheart?" she asked, brows knitted with concern. "You didn't get the job?"

"Stop, Gran," I said, pushing her hand away. "You'll ruin Grandad's hanky."

"Oh, don't be stupid, honey. What do you think it's for?"

"But that's just it," I said, taking a deep breath so I could speak without sobbing. "I *am* stupid. I ran over something on the way home and now my car is broken . . . I got the job. But I'm not going to take it. I'll call them tomorrow and let them know."

"Why? Why don't you want it?"

"I dunno," I replied. "Just a . . . bad feeling."

"I've learned a few things over the course of my long life, Queenie," Gran said, sighing. "Things aren't always what they appear to be." She took my jaw gently between her thumb and middle finger like she always did when she wanted me to pay attention, forcing me to look at her directly. "You don't have a lot of options right now, and this job might be just what you need."

"Sorry, but I just can't do it."

"You need to take this job," she said. "Queenie, I know it was painful when your mother left, but that was a long, long time ago. You were four . . . I know it's hard to trust people, let them in . . . I know you're lonely, sweetheart."

"What does that have to do with anything?" I mumbled, wiping my nose on the back of my sleeve.

"These things can make it hard to move on," she said, resting a cool hand on my cheek. "Even when we know we have to." I closed my eyes and sagged deeper into the sofa. She was right. New situations terrified me. That's probably all it was, the deep sense of foreboding about the job. It was strange: when I was there, in the restaurant, it was as if a spell was cast over me making me want to be there, making me feel something unfamiliar and hopeful. But once I left, the doubts rolled in, the fears. The sense that I was going nowhere fast.

"Okay, okay," I backtracked. "You're right. I'm scared. I'm scared of getting stuck there, scared of never doing anything with my life." She nodded. I felt bad. She had put up with a lot of worry from me over the years. "I wish Harvey was still around," I said. Gran glanced hard at me, like maybe I'd lost the plot. "To fix the car." Harvey the mechanic had a garage in the neighborhood for nearly fifty years, until last year, when he'd passed away after a long illness. Gran and I went to his funeral.

"Oh, sure," she said, as if relieved. As if she knew that by making this dull, random statement, I was telling her I was still with her. She swiped at my under-eyes with the hanky again. "I do miss Harvey. He sure knew how to fix cars and never charged more than a person could afford. Such an honest person." She stared off into space for a moment, forehead creased, thinking. "And then there's Wyatt Jones," she murmured under her breath, shaking her head. "Well. I guess we'll just see, won't we?"

"How do you know a guy like him, anyway?" I asked, thinking of Mrs. Lal's disapproving expression when I mentioned his restaurant.

"It's good you went for the interview, dear." Gran patted my leg before rising to her feet. "Oh! You know . . ." Her eyes widened. "I've just thought of something. Can't think why it never occurred to me before, but I guess we had Harvey right close by . . . Anyway, there's an old friend of mine—haven't talked to him in years. He might be able to help. With the car repairs."

"An old friend?" I asked. "Gran. Don't I know all your friends?"

"Not by a longshot, sweetie. I've got all sorts of secrets." She twinkled in my direction. Gran spoke cryptically like this sometimes—I'd always assumed she was just teasing. But now, having discovered she knew Wyatt Jones, and here she was bringing up some mysterious car mechanic . . . I wondered if Gran really did have secrets. "You'll find Manny and his shop very interesting. Can't think why I never brought you there before," she said lightly, which I knew meant she was hiding something. "Now go walk Daisy before dinner, and I'll put those rolls you like in the oven. We are celebrating, after all." Gran moved toward the kitchen.

"Celebrating?"

"Your new job, Queenie." She shook her head. "Really," she muttered to herself, "young people don't know how good they have it."

Anxiety flared again at the thought of showing up for work on Wednesday at Vista Mar. I was looking down the barrel at yet another stupid, dead-end job that would sap my energy and end me right back where I was now: broke, depressed, exhausted. The sparkle I'd detected in the atmosphere of Vista Mar was likely a misreading, wishful thinking. By this time next week, I was sure I'd have compiled several more kitchen horror stories to add to my collection. Macho line cooks making comments about my ass or my legs. Customers blaming me for a slow kitchen or their own bad day.

Did I not know how good I had it? I would be turning thirty in a few short months. God, I felt like a mess. I pushed the toes of my black leather boots into the shag carpet as if I could grind all my frustration and regret into the fibers.

The familiar shuffle of pots and pans drifted through to where I sat in the living room. Daisy, Gran's caramel-colored corgi-lab mix, trotted in, planted herself at my feet, and whined. I patted my lap, thinking a snuggle would be nice, but she refused with a shake of her curly ears, then stared hard at me with hopeful brown eyes. I guessed it was time to go for a walk. "You better get going to be back in time," Gran called over the sound of water running in the kitchen sink.

Daisy knew the way to the trail down the bluffs. She was so good I didn't even put her on the leash. Recently, Gran had been asking me to walk her more often. Sometimes we went together, but it wasn't like when I was younger when the two of us would spend entire days roaming the bluffs in search of herbs for Gran's remedies, like the brown sagebrush liniment that fixed even the worst muscle aches and mugwort tincture to calm the nerves.

The street was quiet but for the windows, the usual twitch of the next-door neighbor's lace curtains. She seemed always to be monitoring our comings and goings. A marine layer was moving in off the water, but it wasn't yet affecting visibility. A ways down the street, just around the curve, a man I'd never seen before got out of a black sedan holding a briefcase. He paused, patting the pockets of his suit jacket. Turning back as I passed, he aimed his keys at the BMW, which locked with a beep. I waved, thinking he must be a new neighbor and not half bad-looking. He nodded. Detecting a flicker of interest in his expression, I wondered if he was attached. His house sure looked like a family affair: modern, at least three bedrooms, probably. Most of the houses in the neighborhood were owner-occupied, but I thought I remembered a for rent sign on this property a few weeks back. The houses were varied in the neighborhood. Some of the small ones had been built as early as the late twenties, like Gran's bungalow, while others were larger and more modern. Many were mansions with glass fronts that I didn't even really feel classy enough to look at. I'd changed into jeans, running shoes, and a hoodie, which I now zipped up to the top, burrowing my chin into the neck. A chill breeze made everything feel clean and fresh. My spirits lifted just a little with each step. Walking outside in nature always helped. It didn't hurt I had stew and fresh baked bread to look forward to. Truth was, I loved living with Gran. She took care of me, and I liked to think I took care of her, too. Most of my friends didn't understand, saw me living with her as a failing, because in the United States extended families don't usually live all together. But Gran was originally European, from a Roma family, so our situation never seemed odd to her. She and my grandfather had raised me. My dad was never in the picture. I don't think he ever knew about me. Mom was in law school when she accidentally got pregnant with me, and super busy, so she moved back in with Gran and Grandad before I was born. Gran took care of me while Mom studied for the bar exam and worked as a paralegal with the District Attorney's office. She was planning to go into environmental law. But then a few weeks after my fourth birthday, she left. I don't know why. She had been jumpy and irritable, not her nature at all, and then she was gone. Just . . . disappeared. Gran said Althea loved me very much and didn't have a choice about leaving . . . which I've never understood. Or, rather, I don't even know for sure if she left or if something happened to her . . . there was a dark feeling around it all. I just knew she wasn't there anymore. My grandparents didn't like to talk about it. If I asked about her, they said wherever she was, she was missing me.

Daisy turned onto the steep, narrow path leading down to the dirt track, and I followed. Sandy soil crunched under my feet. We passed the sprawling bay laurel in odorous yellow bloom. I plucked a leaf, putting it in my pocket for luck. Gran had special knowledge of Southern California's flora and fauna, though she was born six thousand or so miles away in the mountains bordering France and Germany. When I was young, we'd walked this path almost every day and I'd pester her to tell me about the people who had made Southern California their home for thousands of years. The Tongva had a thriving village here at the base of the bluffs. After rains, Gran and I would keep our eyes out for fossilized shells from when this land was underwater, and for rocks and things that looked like old tools. We didn't take them, but left them where they were, or put them under an old coastal oak that overlooked a view all the way to downtown and the mountains beyond. Whenever I pass that tree, even now as an adult, I always greet it with respect. I loved to hear Gran tell the myths about gods and tricksters, and after she told one story I'd beg for more.

Weywot was the god of the sky. He was created by Quaoar when he sang the song of creation, my favorite one began. When she told these stories, I often wondered what the land had looked like and felt like before so many of the native grasses and plants were destroyed, and before the LA River was encased in concrete after the big flood in '38. I guess that's what those stories did; they made non-human things like plants and animals seem important, connected ... vulnerable. They made you feel like it wasn't all about you.

A small lizard skittered across the trail, reaching safety under a bush before Daisy could register its flight. She loved to chase after them on her short legs, ridiculous ears flapping. Her efforts never came to anything. As I walked along, only half paying attention to what the dog was doing, I thought about the short story I'd been working on. It had been a long time since I'd felt excited about a writing project. But I had a good feeling about this one. The idea had come to me in a dream, and I was still working it out. It was about a surfer who goes out religiously every morning for years, often seeing pods of dolphins in those wee hours, and sometimes swimming with them. One day he begins to feel like he can understand what they're saying, not like they're speaking English, but that he can understand dolphin language. He feels like he's going crazy. The problem is, they're giving him a warning about a massive earthquake that will devastate the entire coast, and he's not sure he can afford to ignore it. So, his options are either look like a wacko who thinks he can talk to dolphins and possibly save millions of lives—or just let it all play out. I wasn't sure yet whether Bud was losing his mind or if he could actually talk to dolphins, which means I hadn't really figured out what kind of story it was.

I sidestepped to avoid a lump of coyote scat. Cottonwood leaves shivered and glinted overhead. Chorus frogs chirped in the murky creek down the bluff. Daisy ran off into the masses of yellow and purple wildflowers. She returned covered head to toe in sickly sweet pollen, with a stick in her mouth. She looked at me pleadingly. I threw it for her and she disappeared again. Should the surfer confide in his best friend? He could bring her out to see for herself and then . . .

The wind was against us on our way back. Stronger, with a damp edge. A bank of thick moisture obscured the setting sun. The walk had cleared my head. Soup. Bread. Sleep. I had a lot to look forward to. Maybe the sparkle I'd sensed at the restaurant was real, and things really would be different this time. Maybe Vista Mar would be a fresh start. I shivered, thinking of poor Bud knowing a big quake was coming but unable to warn people for fear of them thinking he was unhinged. I quickened my pace. Suddenly, all I wanted was to be home.

A cozy waft of woodsmoke hit me when we turned onto the street from the path. Gran might've started a fire, but the bungalow was dark. Odd. With the sun behind the clouds like they were, she would have turned on some lights. A feeling like something was wrong clutched at my throat and I broke into a run. The front door was wide open.

We never used the front door, always the kitchen one.

Daisy on my heels, I dashed up the steps, pausing in the doorway when I caught sight of the overturned cart. One crystal tumbler lay half-submerged in mustard shag by my foot. My eyes followed the line of upended chrome and glass to the other side of the room. Grandad's decanter lay smashed into sparkling shards on the brick hearth, where a fire blazed.

"Gran!" I shouted, my breath coming in short gasps. No answer. I crossed the living room in two strides. The kitchen was bathed in quiet blueish dusk. I could hear the stew simmering a little too hotly on the stove, thick bubbles splattered against the lid, making it jump and dance.

Gran was collapsed on the tile floor, curled on her side like she was sleeping. I froze. For a moment my vision faded blank, then clicked back into focus. I was vaguely aware of Daisy whining, letting out short, high-pitched barks. Gran's hair cascaded silver over her face. Her red cloth flats were still on her small feet, and her light gray skirt wound around her legs like a sheet. Her arms were cast out as if she'd tried to catch herself. Daisy looked from me to Gran, me to Gran, then tentatively put her nose into the crease of Gran's neck, settled into a crouch, and began to whimper.

The lack of response from my grandmother's body was like a wall I couldn't pass through. A wall she had passed through, and me on the other side pounding with both fists to be let in. In my blind panic, I somehow managed to call 911 on the landline. I grabbed the phone off the counter, dragging the cord across the kitchen floor. With the receiver wedged between my shoulder and ear, I started CPR, rounds of chest compressions followed by breaths administered to parted, slack lips, still warm but growing increasingly cold. I remembered the smooth rubber, almost powdery skin of the dolls we learned on in a high-school lifeguard training course. At some point, I must have known that it was futile. All was still but for the murmur of the dispatcher on the other end of the line. I kept hold of Gran's hand after checking her pulse one last time, Daisy wedged between us. I was sitting on the floor beside her in the semi-dark when the first responders came, the only light from the glow of my phone and the murky dusk outside the windows. They came in through the front door, radios blaring scratchy nonsense words, and turned on all the lights, a shock to the eyes. One of them came around behind me, grasped my arms, lifted me to standing. He led me through to the living room by the elbow. I was in a dream state, not fully aware but in an in-between place, like I was experiencing myself from a distance.

"Do you have a leash?" he asked. "We need the room cleared." I pointed to the floor by the door where I'd dropped Daisy's leash. Careful not to disturb the surrounding broken glass, he retrieved the leash and went to get Daisy.

I stood there, surveying the room through bleary eyes. At first glance, it looked much the same as it had an hour earlier. To think that someone had broken into the house and attacked my elderly grandmother was . . . unthinkable. My stomach turned over as I imagined her puttering around the kitchen, stirring the pot, sipping from her glass of rioja; someone knocking on the front door . . . or maybe just opening it? Had it been locked when I left? We never used it. I had no idea.

The cushions were neatly arranged on the sofa, the hand-crocheted lace doilies over the backs of the two armchairs hadn't been disturbed. Some papers had fallen off Gran's desk in the corner. The small blue and brass steamer trunk beside it was shut like always, but when I looked closer, I saw the lock looked banged up, and there were scratches in the paint around it, like someone had tried to open it. I'd always been curious to know what she kept in there. When I'd asked about it, she replied that it just held old papers and things, nothing important.

My relief that the intruder had not been able to open it gave way to rage.

Those were Gran's private things. How dare someone invade her home and disturb her belongings. I was still standing there staring at the trunk when the man returned carrying an agitated Daisy. He handed her over to me. She felt warm and heavy in my arms, a bundle of life. "You live here?"

I nodded.

"You'll have to be out of the house for at least a few hours while they look everything over," he said. An officer in uniform walked in the front door and through to the kitchen, closely followed by a woman in slacks and a dark jacket who took photos with a camera as she went. "They'll probably ask you to go down to the station to give a statement."

Beyond him, out the open door, the dark curve of the street was puddled with faint yellowish light from the lamps above. I had the odd sensation that I wasn't inside looking out, but outside looking in.

Four

I awoke on Wednesday morning with a deep sense of foreboding and a splitting headache. Just two days had passed since Gran was pronounced dead, but time didn't matter. I was due to start at Vista Mar that day.

I sat up and swallowed several of the Advil I'd taken to keeping by my bed for the headache, not because I thought they would help, but because it was a thing to do, a measure to take. The result didn't matter. All that mattered was getting from one moment to the next without succumbing to the abyss her absence had invited into my life. The terror inspired by how I'd found her and not knowing what had happened.

Those days following Gran's death were like that; doing things because they seemed like the thing to do, not because they would help. Nothing helped. Nothing connected to anything else. When I ate, I didn't taste. My hand holding a fork, moving food to my mouth, seemed like a separate entity, totally external. My stomach miles away from my mouth, like another country. When I breathed there was no smell, no air, only a void. Everything seemed disjointed, too large, loud, and close, like a fever dream.

I did not plan to show up for work. How could I?

And yet, I couldn't not show up.

Now, more than ever, I needed the money. All the cash I had was in the stupid Russian doll on the shelf, and it wasn't much. I didn't really think someone was going to break in again—it was a freak accident, a robbery that hadn't amounted to anything for whoever the thief had been. But still, an abundance of caution had made me take the doll, which contained at least a hundred dollars in small bills, off the shelf the night before and stash it under the sink behind the cleaning supplies.

I groped my way, eyes crusted and blurry, from bed to bathroom. The morning light streaming in the windows seemed like a personal affront to the eddies of grief and guilt swirling inside of me. My image in the bathroom mirror was puffy and blank-looking, the circles under my eyes as dark as the bruise I'd glimpsed on Gran's right temple when they'd asked me to officially identify her body. It was as if my own face had been removed and put back on askew. Daisy was with me, though, thank god. I think she felt worse than I did. She followed me around like a shadow and hadn't touched her kibble. I'd been putting off as much as I could, retreating to bed when I got overwhelmed.

Of course, I'd been to the police station on Sunday night, but they let me return home around two o'clock in the morning. I'd called my uncle in San Diego to give him the news. He, of course, didn't want me to stay in the house.

"What if the murderer comes back?" he'd said after a long, shocked pause. That was typical Randy, deal with the immediate crisis first, feelings later.

"It wasn't a murderer, Randy," I'd answered, not entirely convinced. What if they were someone I knew, someone who knew I might have drugs? What if my old mistakes had something to do with Gran's death? I pushed those thoughts away. Arlo was the one with a connection to a dealer. He was the one with questionable associates. I was peripheral to that whole thing, a bystander. Not an innocent one, exactly, but not a person of particular interest. "Some delinquent broke in hoping to steal something and Gran had the bad luck of getting in his way."

That was, essentially, what the police had told me. Their investigation had turned up relatively little. From the way things looked, Gran had answered the front door. Whoever was waiting outside pushed their way in, upending the cart to get past Gran, knocked her over in the kitchen, then went about their business, leaving her there to die. Gran's bedroom showed signs of having been rifled through, but no fingerprints. The blue trunk in the living room had been forced open, its contents disturbed. I'd never seen inside, so couldn't tell the detective if anything was missing. The cops said it was most likely a random breaking and entering gone wrong—they thought the house was empty, but it wasn't. They didn't know if her assailant had been armed. The signs of struggle showed she'd probably tried to hit the intruder with a cast-iron frying pan. She'd died from being pushed hard across the room. Her skull cracked when it hit the tile floor. Whoever did it was strong . . . But nothing was missing as far as I could tell, not jewelry or cash from the doll on the shelf, which was tucked behind an old-fashioned radio; likely they hadn't noticed it.

Personally, I thought it seemed like they were looking for something. But what? Maybe I'd just read too many crime novels.

"Did your grandmother tell you about any unusual interactions with anyone in the days leading up to the robbery?" the detective assigned to the case in the dark coat had asked, stroking one eyebrow with the eraser of her pencil.

She hadn't been to any events recently. The wetlands conservation meeting with the developers was coming up, which was sure to be contentious, but it hadn't happened yet.

"No."

"Have you?"

"Nothing out of the ordinary, Detective." Then I wondered if that was true. Vista Mar and the people there seemed anything but ordinary. But that was separate from this, and I didn't want to complicate things.

I washed my face with cold water, dressed, forced down a few spoonfuls of plain yogurt. I loaded Daisy into the VW. I'd be gone all evening and didn't want to leave her alone for the day, too. I thought it would be wise to have the car looked at before driving all the way out to Malibu for my first shift at Vista Mar. Gran had written her friend Manny's address, the mechanic she'd mentioned the day she died, on the notepad by the phone. Aside from needing to get my car fixed, I felt compelled to follow up—as if me going to see him had been one of her last requests. Even if this Manny character couldn't fix my car, he was Gran's old friend and he'd want to know what had happened.

Manny's was on a side street near Wilshire Boulevard in one of those nondescript shopping centers where you can get your phone repaired, your cat's nails trimmed, pawn your vintage Rolex, and buy a fresh pressed juice all in one stop. It looked like any mercadito from the front, but it was soon revealed to be a rather large, freestanding building. It was narrow but extended quite a way back. An alley ran between it and the rest of the shopping center, which had blue and green plastic bins lined up against the concrete block wall. After slowly rolling through the crowded parking lot to check it out, I turned right onto the side street, not yet ready to get out of the car and interact with people. There was a fuzzy aura of separation between me and others in those days following Gran's death. I must have still been in shock. I couldn't face people, but I had to.

Around the corner, there was an older woman, her stand up against the blank concrete wall of Manny's, selling elote from one of those street carts with a little grill and a handle you can tilt up to wheel it around. The aroma of butter and charred corn on the cob filled the air. It smelled so good. Daisy must have thought so too because she started doing little jumps to better stick her nose out the window. "All right, all right," I said. When I opened the back door for Daisy, she jettisoned herself through the gap between my body and the edge of the door, landing on the sidewalk. I made a grab for the trailing end of her leash, but she was too quick for me. She proceeded to dash to the elote stand and sit before the woman like a worshipper at the altar of her chosen god. The woman looked over at me, one eyebrow arched beneath her pink sun visor.

"Sorry!" I called. I reached the stand, picked up Daisy's leash.

"She's a good dog," the woman said, nodding. "Look at her." Daisy stood and wagged her tail, tongue hanging from her mouth, a doggy smile on her face. She, indeed, looked like a perfect angel.

"Lo siento," I apologized again.

"What can I say," the woman said. "Dogs like me. They know I feed them." Her round face broke into the most beautiful smile. Her laughing eyes narrowed to slits and the creases at their corners continued across her nose like lines drawn on a map. She leaned down to scratch Daisy behind one ear. The dappling of age spots across her high cheekbones seemed to dance as her face ran through a series of micro-expressions meant for dogs only. "Tienes hambre, eh, perrita?" she said, teasing. Daisy craned her head to lick her hand, which I assume had something delicious on it.

"May I have one, please?" I asked, taking some cash from my wallet.

"Mm-hmm," she said, already shearing kernels from a bright yellow ear of corn into a paper dish. "Crema?"

"Yes, of course." She topped the pile of corn with a white sauce and sprinkled it with paprika and shredded cheese.

"Don't share this with your friend," she said, making a face and putting a hand to her stomach. "Too rich. I have something better." From her apron pocket, she pulled a plastic baggie with a handful of what looked like jerky. "My own recipe," she winked. "I sit here, sometimes all day. Need to keep up my energy." She leaned down to offer some to a salivating Daisy, who took it gratefully and very politely. The woman shrugged. "Dogs like it too."

"Thank you," I said, taking a bite of the corn. It was lime and fire and earth. That first bite brought me back into my body. The second smoothed my frayed nervous system. The third caused me to choke back tears.

I hadn't cried since Gran died. Yes, it worried me. But the worry was abstract. What could I do about it? The dull, unrelenting heaviness in my gut, the fog of my thoughts seemed to have taken the place of how I thought sadness would be. Flashes of fury at the unfairness of her death had been my only relief.

"Come visit me again," the elote woman said, settling back down into her chair. "Both of you."

"We'll be back," I managed to say. "That was the best thing I've eaten since . . ." The tears welled behind my eyes, threatening to pour forth. The elote woman nodded, looking up and away, gazing off into the leaves of the stunted little trees lining the quiet street, or at patches of sky, seeming to sense I needed a moment.

I had to pick Daisy up and carry her away. Luckily, it was a short walk to the front door of Manny's. A bell tinkled above us as we entered the dim quiet interior. It took a few seconds for my eyes to adjust. When they did, I saw it looked more like an old-fashioned general store you see in movies than a typical modern-day convenience store. Wooden shelves painted Greek island blue ran along the walls, filled with items that somehow didn't look dusty. Boxes of soap, toothpaste, and cleaning supplies. Dried beans and rice, spices. One wall held shelves and shelves of books. Another held glass jars of dried plants and roots, votive candles, and cigars. The center of the store held a grouping of three café tables with mismatched chairs. The still air smelled of engine oil, herbs, used paperbacks, and something ancient and unidentifiable. Like feet, but not offensive . . . It was hard to describe.

"How can I help?" said a slow, lazy voice from a dark doorway behind the long wooden counter that spanned the wall opposite. A man stepped forward, wiping his hands on a rag. He was tall. At least six-five, thin as a rail. His head seemed to perch on top of his neck like an overgrown cabbage on a stalk. Was this Manny? His age was entirely indeterminate, but he sure didn't look even in the ballpark of eighty like Gran. "Next time you buy from Señora Chela, feel free to eat here."

"Oh—um, thank you," I said, wondering if I had cheese on my face. I tried to wipe it without being obvious.

"It's good, isn't it?" he said.

"The best."

"Señora Chela does some special magic with that elote," he mused. "And I bet she fed your pup too." I glanced down at Daisy, who did not look as happy about meeting this guy as she was about the Señora. She was hiding behind my leg, looking pointedly back at the door.

"Are you Manny?" I asked. My voice sounded small, weak.

"I am," he said. "My name's on the door and everything."

"My grandmother, Anke Rivers, sent me. She said you might be able to fix my car."

"Anke?" he said, striding over to the café area. He turned one of the chairs backward and plopped down on it. His legs stretched a long way out in front of him, making me think of an oversized daddy longlegs. A shiver went up and down my spine. "Anke Rivers..." He tucked the rag in the breast pocket of his flannel, leaned his elbows on the back of the chair. "Right, she married a guy named Rivers." He seemed to be talking to himself. "I haven't heard that name in... some years. How is Anke?" My stomach lurched. Of course, I knew it would come up, but that didn't make it any easier.

"She recently... died," I said. Saying passed away or passed on didn't feel right. The way Gran went wasn't peaceful, but to say she was murdered or killed also seemed wrong. She died. It was a simple, clear, inarguable fact.

Manny drew in a deep breath. He studied me with concern.

"I'm sorry for your loss," he said. "She was wonderful."

"Yeah... So, you were friends?"

He nodded, answering even more slowly than he'd been speaking before. "Anke was a friend, yes." He tapped the back of the chair, taking in the news. "You need help with your car?" he asked, finally. "I'm happy to take a look at it, on the house, for an old friend."

"You haven't even seen it yet," I said. "What if it needs an expensive part or something?"

"No matter," he replied. He glanced down at Daisy, who was still cowering behind my leg. "She okay? Don't ask me to fix your dog, they are an utter mystery to me. You look like her, by the way."

"My dog?"

"No, of course not. You look like your grandmother."

Manny guided me to a room off the garage, which was behind the store area. As we walked the long hallway, he rambled. "Q works during the day in the back room, through here, he knew Anke, too, and will want to meet you. He's kind of like my father but not my father. You know how that is, right? Q, we have a visitor!"

The room glittered in the light of fixtures of all shapes and sizes. They hung from the ceiling and stood on the floor and were attached to the walls, shedding golden light over the poured concrete floor, walls painted the color of river clay, and the very old man who sat on a stool weaving the most enormous fishing net I'd ever seen. It flowed from his fingers like tides. Sections of it hung on random hooks on the walls and over wall lamps and it was layers and layers and layers deep, mounds upon mounds of intricate fibers. "Wow..." I breathed. The scene was so foreign to anything I'd ever seen, it took a minute to take it all in. It was like entering another dimension.

The man didn't look up from his work, just nodded slowly and continued passing twine in a complicated pattern of knots around itself. His source lay at his feet, a massive pile of thin sand-colored rope coiled into a round.

"Hello, Queenie," he said, meeting my gaze.

"Hi, wow," I said again, "you're an artist?"

"Of a sort. Sit, sit." He gestured to another low stool I hadn't noticed before. "You may wait here while Manny tends to your vehicle."

"Thank you," I said. There was a sense of peace infusing the room, which seemed to make Daisy feel right at home. And me too. I lowered myself onto the stool, which was surprisingly comfortable, even supportive. For the first time in a long time I felt, if not happy, at ease. Daisy sniffed around for a few minutes, then found a nest in a tangle of rope in the corner and slept.

"Busted gas tank. Lucky it didn't spring a leak," Manny said, coming back inside sometime later twirling a wrench in one pie-plate hand and dangling a thin white thread between the thumb and forefinger of the other. Time was strange in that room. "The muffler was hanging on by a thread. You didn't happen to try to hold it together with dental floss, did you?"

I blushed and decided not to answer the question. "Can you fix it?"

"Already done," Manny said.

"Done?" I asked. How long had I been in this room?

"Replaced the gas tank and the exhaust system."

"That sounds expensive."

"Not for you. This one's on me," Manny said, "for the dearly departed. Besides, the body's all rusted out underneath. Not worth it to anyone to try and fix that. You'll need a new one soon." I sighed on the inside, even as I thanked him for the free work. The thought of monthly car payments made me want to crawl under Q's fantastic net and die. Manny pocketed the wrench and the dental floss, wiping his hands together like he was done with something. I should have been relieved to get on my way but found myself feeling disappointed it hadn't taken longer. There was something about the old man working away like he had all the time in the world . . .

"Thank you," I said. "Thank you very much, that's very generous." I didn't like to feel indebted, but in my circumstances, I couldn't afford to refuse the offered kindness. I just hoped I wouldn't regret it.

"No matter," Manny said. He turned to Q. "Did you know this is Anke's granddaughter?" Q nodded. His shimmering white hair was illuminated by a wrought iron chandelier over his head. "And that Anke has left us?" Q looked up at me, his irises were so dark they appeared black. His obsidian eyes captured pinpoints of light from around the room.

"She will . . . be missed," he said.

"Manny mentioned you were fond of my grandmother?" I asked. He nodded without raising his eyes. "How did you know her?"

Q didn't answer. I looked at Manny, who shrugged. "A story for another time," he said.

I was happy he seemed to expect me to return, though I wasn't sure what to make of him. Something about the place, I liked it there, felt relaxed. Just then, Daisy, who obviously shared my feelings about Manny's, awakened and stretched, shook herself, then wandered out the door, not bothering to see if I would follow.

"Where you headed today?" Manny asked.

"Home, then I start a new job this afternoon."

"Oh yeah?" he said, seeming interested. "Whereabouts?"

"Vista Mar. Over on the coast."

Manny raised his eyebrows.

"What?" I asked.

"Nothing," he replied. "Just . . . careful. That place has a reputation."

"For what?"

"Oh, Wyatt Jones. He's a character." More vague warnings about Wyatt and the restaurant. I wanted to inquire further, but Manny called to Daisy and shooed me out the door. I looked over at Q who was dozing in his seat, twine resting in his lap. "Come, I'll show you what I did with the car. Will there be a memorial for Anke?" Manny asked.

"Sunday," I said. "We have an appointment with Gran's lawyer about her will on Friday."

"Your mom's coming?" My stomach clenched.

"You know Althea?" I answered, my voice sounding high and far away.

"Sure," he said. "We went to law school together."

"You went to law school?"

"Law school dropout," he said, not seeming upset about it at all. "Wasn't for me." He smiled. Manny's eyes were a curious color, a sort of violet ring around the iris with cool green around the pupil. Strange eyes.

"Althea's been gone for years. I haven't seen her since I was four," I said, bracing myself for his reaction. But he didn't seem surprised, didn't give me a pitying look like most people when I told them. "Do you want to come?" I asked. "To the memorial." As we walked to the car, which was parked just inside the rolling door that opened onto the street, I realized I really did want him to come.

The aroma of grilled corn wafted in on the breeze. Daisy, who had wandered away while we were talking to explore the building, came into the garage all excited. Maybe thinking she was going to have another visit with Señora Chela.

"Yes, of course I'll come," he replied.

"Will Q come, too?" That peace, I wanted more of it.

Manny shook his head. "Not likely. He's pretty tied up with that project. But Señora Chela might." He chuckled at his own joke as he climbed in the driver's seat and started the engine. Not even a hint of a rattle. He handed me the keys. Daisy jumped in and sat expectantly in the passenger seat. I took a scrap of paper from my bag, wrote down the address of the house, handed it over. If I couldn't trust Manny, well, now he knew where I lived. I got in the car, closed the door, opened the window.

"Until Sunday. Oh, and Queenie?"

"Yeah?"

"If you have trouble, don't hesitate to call." He ripped off a piece of the paper I'd given him, beckoned for me to give him my pen, and wrote down a series of numbers. "Good luck at Vista Mar," he said. "You call anytime, okay?"

"Got it," I said. "Thanks again!" As I drove away, I wondered if he meant trouble with the car or trouble at Vista Mar.

Five

I walked in the front door of Vista Mar at four on the dot. A crackly live recording of "Grandma's Hands" played in surround from carefully concealed speakers around the room, causing the now-constant pit in my stomach to expand. Without thinking, I slipped behind the bar, bent to surreptitiously nudge the knob on the volume down while keeping an eye out for Rita lurking at the host station. Rising to stand, I came face to face with the bartender.

"Hey," he said. "Not a Bill Withers fan?"

"It's not that—" I protested, turning red. Never had I ever done something so bold on my first day at a job. "Sorry. It reminds me of . . . someone," I said, attempting to rally, failing miserably. "I'm supposed to start today."

"Yup," he said, gesturing to the table he'd laid out, all perfect angles and spaces. I wouldn't have been surprised if he handed me a ruler. "Here's your model."

"Wha-at?" I was confused.

"You've done this before?" he asked. "You can set a table, carry some plates, serve some drinks?"

"Uh, sure," I said, heartbreaking music and embarrassing memories forgotten. "Is someone going to train me?"

"Nobody here but you and me," he replied. "Tell you what. If you get stuck, you'll find me right there where you're standing." He gestured behind the bar with one well-muscled, tattooed arm.

"What's your name?" I asked, crossing my arms over my chest to show him I wasn't intimidated. "Or do I have to figure that out for myself, too?"

He scowled, causing his striking features to appear even more unapproachable. "Well, I guess you can call me whatever you want," he said dryly. "Like I said when we met the other day, people call me Pirate."

I raised my eyebrows at him. "That's your real name?"

"Is Queenie your real name?"

I smiled. His dark eyes were kind despite his brusque manner, and he had, after all, defended me from Rita the day of my interview. "My full name's

Regina, but I've always been called Queenie." I looked around. "So yeah, it is my real name. Where can I put my stuff?"

Pirate dropped a rag on one of the bare tables. "Through the kitchen doors and to the right. Use any of the lockers back there."

There was a commotion behind the host station, muffled voices from behind the closed door leading up to Wyatt Jones's office.

"No!" An angry voice came through clearly. There were some garbled words I couldn't make out and Wyatt's murmured response, then the heated voice again. "You need to do something, Wyatt. People are going missing."

The door opened and Shen, the accountant I'd met briefly at my interview, stalked out. He stopped short when he saw me. I badly wanted to ask him what was going on. Shen raised an eyebrow in Pirate's direction, threw up his hands in disgust, shouted, "I'm out," and left. I drew in a deep breath, looked sideways at Pirate, wondering what, exactly, I'd gotten myself into, taking a job at this place. People were . . . missing? What people? Pirate picked up a clean towel, held it out to me.

"You staying or going?" he asked. I sucked in a breath, thought of my almost empty Russian doll, released the breath, and took the towel.

Toward the end of my shift, which included waiting on six parties all night long, but also included tips totaling three hundred and fifty-three dollars, Wyatt emerged from his office. He acted like nothing had happened earlier. He was wearing a well-cut suit that looked like it had been pressed five minutes before. He ambled over to the cash register behind the bar and waved me over.

"We had some very important customers in here tonight, new girl," he said, "real VIPs. You did well." I nodded, choosing to ignore his referring to me as "girl." Okay then, whatever. It wasn't a hard job, and I went home with a wad of cash in my pocket. "Wednesdays are slow, there'll be more people tomorrow. Rita will be here, and another server."

"Okay," I said.

It felt natural to edge away from Wyatt, despite his apparent amiability. It was the business with Shen. He had been so distraught. People going missing was never good. Was most always very bad, in fact. Forget it, I told myself, it's none of your business. Just make as much money as possible and move on. No need to get involved. But in the next moment, Wyatt forced me to choose sides. He took the drawer out of the register and counted out twenties into a pile in front of me. An extra two hundred dollars for—what? He placed his hand over the bills.

"What Shen said before... It never happened, okay? If you're going to work here, you need to be a team player. We take care of our own, right, Pirate?" The scar above Wyatt's lip twitched. I wondered how Pirate got his name. Was he the underdog leader of important rebellions kind of pirate who steals for a good cause? Or the scourge of the seven seas evil type? The one thing I knew about him for sure was that he was impossible to read.

I looked over at the bartender. He put a tray of glasses in the dishwasher, shut the door, pressed some buttons. Water rushed into the machine below the counter.

"I can't remember the last time I saw Shen around here," Pirate said. He gazed at me, blank-faced. Wyatt slid the money toward me with his fingertips. I'd been broke for so long. I took the pile of bills, folded it up, and tucked it into my apron pocket.

"Who's Shen?" I said.

Six

Gran's lawyer's office was in a brick building downtown, not too far from Central Library. My Uncle Randy had driven up from San Diego and met me on the steps outside. Above the doorway was a carved frieze featuring a stone-winged angel riding a dragon.

Althea's younger brother Randy's close-cropped hair had gone entirely gray since the last time I saw him. He was the spitting image of Grandad as I remembered him when I was growing up, taking me on adventures to the park and the beach on weekends, picking me up after school, a man of medium build with light brown skin and dark, kind eyes that crinkled at the corners even as they regarded you sternly. Randy and Althea both had Gran's high cheekbones and strong, straight nose. My uncle, an officer in the Navy, had followed in his dad's footsteps and joined the military straight out of high school. He'd maintained the habit of running and working out every day, even after switching over to a desk job, and had always been in perfect shape despite his dietary habits that tended toward the bacon, eggs, and sausage end of the spectrum. Grandad had died of acute cardiac arrest after years of high cholesterol and out of control blood pressure, and Gran had confided in me that she worried about him following in his dad's footsteps in that respect, too. Randy greeted me, gave me a squeeze. When he did, I had to hold back tears, looking away and trying to think and talk about anything other than why we were there. It was like there was so much to say and process, but I wasn't ready. I didn't want to say anything meaningful, and Randy seemed to intuit this, though I'm sure he was enduring his own version of shock and grief. We chatted about the traffic and the green juice he stopped for on the way. He grimaced when he said *green juice*.

"That would have made Gran happy," I said, "you eating right."

"I know, that's why I got it. Wasn't too bad," he said, glancing skyward, patting his nonexistent gut. "Could get used to eating more bougie cow food, I guess. Anyway, my nerves couldn't take another cup of coffee. Not today." We proceeded into the building without commenting on the details of why we were there or what had happened. We entered the cool dark interior of the building's foyer and pressed the button for the elevator. On the way up, we talked about the weather.

We stepped off the elevator on the fifth floor, followed the signs for suite 502. The waiting room of the office was empty when we walked in. There was a tall potted ficus beside a receptionist's desk. The draft from the door made the leaves flutter when we entered. It smelled like polished wood and dust, like you'd imagine a lawyer's office would have smelled fifty years ago. I imagined Gran had felt at home here. Ben Schwartz, however, who popped his head in from the main office, was not the elderly lawyer I expected given the decor. He looked a little older than me, maybe early thirties. Tall, medium build, shaggy dark hair, glasses, tweed blazer and jeans.

"Come on in," he said, waving us over. I looked down. A dime glinted on the hardwood floor between my feet. I picked it up and put it in my pocket before following Randy and the adorable lawyer inside. The lawyer, who asked us right off to call him Ben, held the door for us and shook each of our hands as we walked through. We sat in comfortable chairs around one end of a long table in the center of the room. Ben went to his desk and picked up a thick folder, then took the seat to my right.

"Mrs. Rivers was a friend of my grandmother's," he said, making eye contact with each of us. "It's how I got to be her lawyer."

I liked how he said he *got* to be her lawyer, like he'd won a prize. It was how I felt about Gran as well. He rubbed his cheek absently, seeming to want to say just the right thing. Randy, probably wanting to put him at ease, said, "It's okay, Ben. We're in this together, right?"

Ben smiled and visibly relaxed. "I just wanted to say that I'm sorry she went . . . the way she did," he said. "She was a wonderful person." I had been too preoccupied before to notice the sunlight streaming in the tall windows or the delicious smell wafting from a plate of walnut-studded cinnamon rolls in the center of the table. Ben stood and went to a sideboard where a silver samovar stood beside a shelf of china plates and saucers.

"Tea?"

Randy and I nodded. I was just glad I would have somewhere to put my hands, something to look at. Steam rose as Ben poured tea from the ornate spout into each cup, filling the room with a warm, earthy scent. I touched the dime in my pocket. When Gran found dimes, she'd said her angels were trying to tell her something. What's the message, Gran? I wondered. If I somehow could have known, could have had one more day with her, what would we have done? What would I have asked her? It was an irrational thought, and not comforting.

Ben read the will slowly, stopping every so often to make sure we were following. When he said Gran left the bungalow to me, Randy nodded affirmingly and squeezed my hand. She had left Grandad's medals to Randy, and her savings. To Althea, the oddest bequest: A deck of tarot cards, which Gran wrote were in the blue steamer trunk. Also included was a key to the lock. *Why?* I mouthed. Randy shrugged, appearing equally mystified. I hadn't known Gran was into esoteric stuff. Apparently, neither had he. Ben said one of us could assume guardianship of Althea's inheritance. He'd run a search for her and turned up nothing. My heart flipped. Mom had disappeared so thoroughly. Was she even alive? Gran didn't have an answer for me the few times I'd asked about her growing up, so I'd stopped asking. A therapist I'd seen a few times told me that people like me, people with unresolved issues like a missing parent, often become very good at compartmentalizing. I'd gotten used to living in a version of the world where there was no reason to ask about my mother. It just was what it was. Now, Gran's death was making it impossible not to wonder. And I didn't know the first thing about being a homeowner. There was no mortgage, but I'd have to pay property taxes and... My scattered, panicked thoughts were interrupted by Ben Schwartz shuffling through a stack of papers and passing Randy and I each a sealed envelope.

"She left personal letters," he said. The paper, when I took it out, smelled of sweet hay, rose, and sandalwood. Tears were streaming down my cheeks. Ben passed me a box of tissues. I took a handful, wiping at my eyes as I read Gran's narrow, slanted handwriting:

Dearest Queenie,

If you're reading this, I'm already gone. As you are well aware, I've always found it difficult to speak of my past, before I came to America, but it is a part of your history too, and you deserve to know it, all of it. The following is my best attempt to record a complicated series of events. Forgive me if it is missing details, or hard to understand. Please understand this letter is only a beginning. There's so much more, but you'll have to go in search of it.

When I was young I lived in the mountains bordering France and Germany in a stone farmhouse with my mother and father, two younger twin sisters, and an older brother. As you may know, throughout the world there's quite a stigma attached to the Roma people. In part, this is because in order to protect our heritage and lineage, many families live apart from non-Roma. People don't trust what they don't know. But my family sent us children to school in the village, and we built a reputation for ourselves as honest and capable. The men in my family were horse trainers and breeders, as well as talented mechanics. For a month in the summer season we had a tradition of going back to the old ways and we traveled in a caravan along with extended family, to do work for patrons who lived on outlying farms. To earn extra money, especially when the horse business was slow, the women told fortunes. They read the tarot or tried using a nail strung on a length of thread. People were usually satisfied with the readings, often grateful, but sometimes when we were on the road a client would get angry and send their husband or brother after us, and we'd have to pack up camp quickly while a few of the men held off the attackers.

In the summer of 1939, there was a Nazi raid on our camp. How did they find us? I've often wondered. Perhaps some of our friends were not our friends.

They came at night. They brought dogs. By the time our own dogs realized something was wrong, they were already on top of us, breaking down doors and setting things ablaze with sticks from our own fires.

They killed all of the men, my father and older brother included. They killed our dogs. I don't know what they did with the horses. I remember my beautiful gray pony whinnying, terrified, rearing against her stake, her teeth bared, eyes rolling back with raw fear as the powerful flashlights rolled over our belongings, as the Nazis beat anyone who resisted with clubs, the screams, the barking, the heart-rending yelp when my favorite pup, Rakar, tried to defend us and the officers shot him in midair as he leaped from the wagon steps. My mother tried to run with us when she saw my father collapse under a barrage of nightsticks, but their German shepherds cornered us in the woods.

They put me, my little sisters, and my mother in the back of a truck with no windows along with some of the other women and children in our family. We didn't stop. I don't know how long the trip was, maybe days. When we arrived at the camp we were soaked in our own excrement and urine.

I was eleven years old when I entered Dachau with my mother and sisters. The girls were much younger, about four or maybe five. In the beginning, we were all together in a bunk room with other women, Jewish and Roma. They shaved our heads. I cried when I saw my long black hair lying on the dirty floor in a tangled dirty heap of other people's hair. I didn't cry when they took my sisters away. They were twins. When they took my sisters away I was angry—It is a terrible story, I know, Queenie. But this and worse happened to countless many. Of the million or so Roma and Sinti in Europe, the Nazis murdered half of them during the Second World War. My mother cried for three days, then gave up. She was already sick. She knew she wouldn't last the winter. At Dachau, they selected twins for medical experiments. We never saw my sisters again.

The day they took them away, I vowed to live, and not just live, but thrive. It was the surest form of revenge I could think of. I don't need to go into more details of what happened to me in my six years at Dachau for you to understand. Just know that my rage, present even now but reduced by time to a dull ache, is what kept me alive in that place.

Liberation came in the form of trucks driven by American soldiers. I first met your grandfather on April 29, 1945. Some of us didn't go out into the yard when they drove up. Though we understood that they were from a different army, that they were not Nazis, we didn't trust right away. We were afraid that they were just more people who would hurt us. I hid under a bunk in the barracks, making a plan in my head that I would wait until dark and then try to escape. There was happy shouting outside. Prisoners were cheering the soldiers for giving them food (many would become very sick, dysentery and vomiting, from eating too much at once after being on a deliberate starvation diet for so long). Cowering under the bunk, I became curious. I was as hungry as the next person. A man walked in, first I saw just his boots, then he came and crouched by the bunk. Half-delirious from malnourishment and existing in a permanent state of terror, I guess I didn't hide very well. He had a handsome, dark-skinned face, no more than a couple of years older than me. He held out a hand to help me up. I didn't know if I could trust him, but I took his hand.

I was sent with a group of other young people to a displaced persons camp, a good one. It was called Foehrenwald. They kept us busy morning to night. I think they didn't want to give us too much time to dwell on what we had been through. Everyone learned a trade. I was in the kitchen, learning to cook. Many of the teachers were from Israel. We learned some Hebrew and some English. It was a healing time. Some people got married and started new lives together. Some of us were offered the choice to go and live in Israel. But Cedric Rivers wrote his name and his mother's address on a piece of paper for me before leaving Dachau. Los Angeles, California. Even though I had no idea what the place was like, the idea of it stuck in my mind like a point of light in all that darkness, that young man who'd been kind to me on Liberation Day, the day the nightmare began to end. In 1947, the US government decided some of us could register to go to the States. I was chosen. I was given a choice between New York and California. I chose California.

The rest, my dear Queenie, is history.

For my sisters, for my mother and father, for my cousins and aunts and uncles . . . for all of them I have done my best to live a good life in spite of its horrific beginnings. I am so grateful for my long life in the United States. You're a talented writer and I thought, maybe, this would give you something to work with. I am leaving you my journals. They're in the blue steamer trunk you've always been so curious about. You have my blessing to tell our family's story.

I love you.

Gran

It took me a few moments to speak once I finished reading. I knew she had survived the camp, that her family were all lost in the war. But her words made it all seem real to me in a way it never had before. Gran was gone. They were all gone. And the very realization of all I had not known fell over me like another death.

"Did she write to you about the concentration camp?" I asked. Randy nodded, looking as wretched as I felt.

Ben looked up from making notes on a legal pad. "When she filed the letters, Mrs. Rivers told me the letters might be upsetting—that they would raise a lot of questions. She said if I felt moved to offer . . . my grandmother is also a survivor. We're Jewish, my grandmother was from Germany originally. Mrs. Rivers, then Ms. Weiss, and my grandmother met in a boarding house here in Los Angeles when they first came to the US after the war, in '48. So if you want to talk, I'm here." His gaze settled on me. "At any point, doesn't have to be today. I'm sure it's a lot to process." These last words came out in a rush, and I nodded, hoping my appreciation showed, because I couldn't speak.

"I only ever knew the bare facts . . ." Randy said slowly. "When I was a kid, I asked if she had siblings, and why I never met my grandparents. Mom said she'd had two sisters and a brother, that they'd died in the war. Her hands shook and her face went white. I rarely asked about them after that."

"I always thought she didn't talk much about being Roma because of losing her family, you know, the memories were too painful," I said, my voice choked. "I never pushed her on it. Now I wish I'd asked more questions."

"Like I said, I'm here if you ever want to talk," Ben said.

I had to be at work later that day, so I headed home to take Daisy out and change. Randy had some business downtown, but he was staying at Gran's until the memorial, so I'd see him later . . . at what was now, apparently, my house.

I had a million thoughts swirling in my head. Gran's letter, the bribe I'd taken from Wyatt Jones (increasingly weighing on me), an email from Arlo saying he missed me and would I meet him for dinner. I hadn't told him about Gran. It wasn't something I wanted to share with him. Seemed to me that was a good enough reason, aside from the obvious ones, not to meet him, but I hadn't answered yet. Also, I'd received another rejection for a story I'd submitted to a few obscure literary journals, and I didn't particularly feel like nodding appreciatively while Arlo went on about his most recent professional developments.

At home, I looked sideways at the open steamer trunk as I walked through the living room like I had been since Gran died. Now I knew I had permission to examine the contents of it, but I wasn't quite ready yet. The police had been over it but hadn't found any fingerprints or anything. None. Nobody witnessed a stranger entering the house, no evidence of who had killed Gran or why. I kicked the wall outside my bedroom door, leaving a small dent in the plaster. It wasn't fair. None of it.

As I was pulling on my running shoes, my phone rang. It was a local number. I answered.

"Regina Rivers?"

"Speaking."

"This is Detective Barnes," said the woman's voice on the other end. Efficient, measured, accustomed to bearing bad news. "I wanted to let you know we've completed our forensic investigation, so we can release your grandmother's personal items back to you."

"Oh, okay," I said. "Did you find anything?"

"No," she said, her curt tone softening. "But with some cases things show up over time, maybe you talk to a neighbor we missed during our investigation and they turn out to be a witness. Keep your eyes and ears open, okay?"

"I will."

"When can you come by the station?"

"I leave for work in an hour. I can stop in on my way."

The plastic bag they gave me held Gran's clothes and shoes, neatly folded. I couldn't bear to look at them too closely. Her jewelry was in a small Ziploc. Tiny gold hoops and the rough-cut black stone in a gold setting she always wore around her neck. I sat in the driver's seat in the parking lot of the police station. I took out the pendant and held it in the palm of my hand. It was heavy and cool. I rubbed the black stone with my thumb. As I sat there, unmoving, it grew steadily warmer. I felt dizzy. When I looked up and out the windshield, the stucco wall of the station in front of me seemed to shimmer and shift, green and violet streaks of light passed before my eyes. Was I high? Having a stroke? I dropped Gran's necklace into the console. The mirage stopped. The wall came back into focus. I was breathing hard. I was going to be late for work.

I called Randy as I drove, put him on speakerphone and told him what had happened.

"It's stress, Queenie," he said. "You've been through hell. You're *not* having a stroke. Sounds like a panic attack. You know, I've been doing some research on trauma—trauma passed down through generations—and with Gran being a survivor and Grandad a war veteran, it's no surprise we all struggle from time to time." I took some slow, deep breaths. *We all struggle some.* Randy's always been so good at hiding his emotions. I had no idea he might struggle with some of the same stuff I did. "Feel better?"

"A little," I said

"Do you want to call out sick? I can meet you at the house in twenty minutes." I thought of all the jobs I'd lost from calling out "sick" or showing up high.

"No," I said, gripping the wheel as I took care to come to a full stop at a stop sign. "I think I'd rather stay busy."

"Okay. I'll see you later."

"Yeah. Okay. Love you."

"And I you, niece. Eyes on the road, hear?"

"Yes sir."

I was grateful for traffic on the 10 and I relaxed a little as I drove. The rain cleared. By the time I reached the Pacific Coast Highway, pockets of blue sky had opened, and sunlight fought the remaining haze. A few pelicans skimmed low over an empty stretch of sand. I wondered what the beaches were like before the Santa Monica Pier was built up with the Ferris wheel and roller coaster and myriad lights and attractions. Before there were houses built practically up to the water and into the cliffs.

There were more cars than I'd seen before in the parking lot at Vista Mar, including an ominous black SUV by the dumpster. When I got out of my car, I took a deep breath of ocean air. The ebb and flow of the waves breaking on the shore was calming. The sun was low in the sky, a haze of moisture gentling its light. I grabbed my bag (avoiding touching the pendant) and walked toward the rear door leading directly to the kitchen from the parking lot.

The doors of the SUV opened in unison. The windows were tinted dark. I hadn't seen there were people inside. A man and a woman in dark suits to match the car stepped out. He was balding. She looked my age, fit. Her hair was pulled back in a tight ponytail. Cops. Instinctively, my mind scanned the contents of my person and car for anything illegal. Nothing. I was clean as a string bean. I've noticed some people can never quite shake the sense of being a ne'er-do-well once they're labeled that way, while others truly aren't bothered by any sense of guilt or inferiority no matter what they do. My heart nearly beat right out of my chest. They're not cops, I told myself, they're just people in a big scary car going to dinner. Except, of course, they weren't. Instead of going to the front door like patrons would, they walked over to me. The guy took a wallet out of his inside jacket pocket, showed me a badge. It showed the emblem of some government organization that went by an acronym that I couldn't make out before he snapped it shut. A holster bulged at his right hip. The wind shifted and the dumpster smell hit me full in the face.

"Do you work here?" asked the one with the ponytail.

"Yes," I said, trying not to gag from the odor of a week's worth of seafood waste, plus anxiety. "But I just started, it's my first week."

"Noticed anything out of the ordinary on the premises?" asked the man with the gun under his jacket.

"I—no." I stumbled over my words. Of course I had.

"If you notice anything, give us a call," said the woman, narrowing her eyes at me. She knows I know something, said my panicked brain. She knows Wyatt Jones bribed me to stay quiet about Shen. My grandmother was murdered last week. I need to find a new job, fast, I thought, trying to meet their eyes and not blink.

"We'd appreciate it if you could keep your eyes peeled for anything unusual." It was almost exactly what Detective Barnes had said over the phone. Why were cops lurking around Vista Mar?

"We can protect people who cooperate with us," the woman said. The man handed me a card: Immigration and Customs Enforcement, Agent Gabe García, Agent Dolores Bresson, followed by a number. It sounded more like a threat than a promise. They turned, got into their vehicle, and drove slowly out of the parking lot. I tore up the card and threw the pieces in the dumpster. But first, I memorized the number. Just in case.

Seven

Rita didn't glance at me when I came through the swinging doors from the kitchen, still tying on my apron. She was on the restaurant phone, speaking in a voice that made it sound like she'd learned to talk by watching morning news shows, a voice that matched her pink blazer. I felt in my pockets to make sure I had pens and a notepad. The other server, a twenty-something named Connor I'd met the last time I worked, nodded in my direction, continuing to set tables out on the patio. I turned to the mirror behind the bar, smoothed down some wayward frizz. I looked innocent enough, not like a liar or someone who would accept a bribe to cover up criminal activity. There was a tingling below my right ear. Rita's eyes were burning a hole in the side of my head. So it was like that. I turned slowly to face her. She looked quickly away and busied herself with the res book.

"Hello, Rita," I said. I wondered how much she knew about Wyatt's shady dealings.

"Queenie," she said, eyes darting anywhere but my face. "Pirate wants you to start on the bar. He's going to be a little late." That explained the lack of tunes.

"Okay," I said, drawing out the word. "Is—"

"He left a list." She seemed in a hurry to be done talking to me. She grabbed a paper off the host station and walked to the bar. Rita slid it across the polished surface, hesitated like she might have something more to say, then turned and walked quickly toward the narrow hallway that housed doors to the customer restrooms. Had I imagined it or were her hands trembling when she handed over Pirate's list?

"Everything okay?" I called after her. Either she didn't hear me or didn't want to answer.

I managed to do my own side work as well as Pirate's before five o'clock, consulting Connor on the location of just a few items, such as the key to the wine cellar, which I had to get from Wyatt. The wine cellar was cool and dim, lined with rough wooden shelves stocked with bottles. The kegs were down there too, directly underneath the bar, I guessed, tracking the lines up the wall to where they went through holes in the ceiling. I was supposed to change out an empty pilsner. Fortunately, the new keg was already in place and I just had to switch out the tap. I guess Pirate knew from my resume that I'd tended bar before. He showed up just as Vista was about to open. I was stocking mineral waters in a small fridge under the bar. He came through the kitchen doors carrying a fresh waft of outdoors. He stopped by me, to survey my work I assumed. I was crouched near the floor, which reeked of spilled beer and citrus cleaner, ferrying glass bottles from milk crate to shelves. Doing his job. His tan work boots were covered in a film of dust up to the hem of his jeans, like he'd been walking on a dirt trail.

"Go for a hike?" I asked, careful to keep my tone light. I stood, wiped condensation off my hands onto a clean towel. I had mixed feelings about Pirate. He was obviously in cahoots with Wyatt. His manner ranged from aloof to dismissive. Still, there was something I liked about him despite all that. He had a shine, a quality of authenticity. Despite evidence to the contrary, I felt I could trust him.

"You an amateur detective?" Pirate asked, holding one of the glasses I'd polished up to the light, his expression blank.

"Writer," I said. "I pay attention to things."

"Written anything I might recognize?" He looked at me sideways.

"Not in a while . . ." I said. The fact was, I had. The *New York Times* had run an essay I wrote about Sunday lunches with Gran and Grandad. I'd written it for class and my professor, who was also my adviser, suggested I send it to an editor she knew.

Growing up, the three of us, Gran, Grandad, and me, would pile into Gran's Buick every Sunday morning and drive somewhere. We called it Destination Sunday, but that was kind of a joke because we never had a destination. We'd pick a place on an old paper map of the city left over from its streetcar, pre-freeway days that Gran had laminated, and go there. We found ourselves in the most unexpected places every single weekend, because if there's anything defining about LA, it's that it is varied. We ate in every kind of mom-and-pop hole in the wall you can imagine—from noodle soups and dim sum to fried chicken and waffles to Korean barbecue to red beans and rice to injera with stewed goat and every iteration of taco you can think of. Before Jonathan Gold, there was Gran. She just didn't bother writing all of it down.

I did, though. I used to bring my notebook and take notes on each neighborhood. I wrote the smells, the light, the sounds. I wrote down what I ordered for lunch and the ingredients I could identify. I wrote about what the people who served us looked like, how they spoke, whether they were friendly or standoffish. I described their clothes, their expressions, and the decorations on the walls. Even the bathrooms. You can tell a lot about a restaurant by its bathrooms.

Because we worked from an outdated map, we sometimes picked a place that looked like a neighborhood and ended up in an underpass. Or we thought we'd be walking along a waterway, but it had been diverted and was no longer anywhere to be seen; but that was part of the fun. I mean, it was sad, but fun. We observed the discrepancies between old city and new. We talked about what it must have been like before, and the ways people used to live.

When Grandad was ill, between his first heart attack and the one that he couldn't recover from, we didn't go. For a year after he died, we didn't go. Then, one Sunday we started up again, just Gran and me.

My first year of college, I took a creative writing class. When my professor suggested I send one of my essays to her editor friend, they ran it and it received some attention, even caught the eye of a literary agent who signed me on. But I couldn't handle the pressure. She was talking essay collection, while I was struggling to keep up with my classes. Then I met Arlo, who was a senior and about to graduate. I got a little too into balancing out the pressure of school and my writing career with a pill here and a few too many drinks there . . . I missed deadlines and meetings . . . The agent dropped me. I dropped school.

"An article in a big newspaper," I said. "It was about eating at restaurants around LA with my grandmother. But that was years ago, and in New York. So short answer is, probably not."

Pirate nodded. "Interesting," he said, opening the fridge, checking the lemon and lime slices. "What are you working on now?" I was internally hemming and hawing when our first customers walked in, giving me a reason not to answer the question. Rita finally emerged from the bathroom and showed them to a two-top on the patio. A man with thinning gray hair in a gray suit and a woman in a navy suit, pearl necklace, and matching earrings. They both looked to be in their late fifties, early sixties.

"Watch yourself with them," Pirate said in a low voice. "That's Melvin Toro, LA County Sheriff. Not sure who she is, but probably someone important. Toro's close with Wyatt. Likes to bring people from the mayor's office here when he wants to butter them up." My gut tensed at the mention of the sheriff.

"More cops," I groaned, not realizing I was speaking aloud. Pirate raised his eyebrows at me. "I—we had a break-in at my Gran's house." I looked down at the floor. "I've been dealing with the police all week."

"Sorry to hear that," he said, picking up the empty ice bucket. "Just bring out the right food while it's still hot and if he calls you little lady or sweetheart, ignore it."

"You mean resist the urge to accidentally dump his soup in his lap?"

Pirate softened so that he looked almost friendly. "Exactly," he said. He headed back to the ice machine in the kitchen. I lifted the bar flap and walked out into the dining room to bring the sheriff some water.

"Calliope," he was saying to the woman as I approached the table with a pitcher of tap water. "How can you expect my department to stay on top of processing rape kits when we don't have the staff and funding to adequately oversee the prisons?" He stopped speaking when I reached them, looking me up and down while I poured water.

"Would you like to start with drinks?" I asked.

"My usual," he said, gesturing to Pirate who was back behind the bar. "He knows."

"Of course," I said. "And for you?" I took the opportunity to study the woman, curious what her job was. She was obviously struggling to stay calm. Her hands were pressed flat on the table in front of her like she was trying not to strangle Melvin Toro. The set of her expressive mouth betrayed distaste for her dinner companion. I waited as she took a deep breath and the tension in her facial muscles released.

"Sauvignon blanc," she said, composure regained. Then added, "Please," as an afterthought.

"You new here, sweetheart?" the sheriff asked me. Calliope gave the reverse nod sexist dinosaurs often evoke from women who aren't sexist dinosaurs themselves.

"Yes, I am," I said, pretending not to notice their tiff. "I started earlier this week." After I described the dishes that weren't on the menu, I stepped away feeling pretty smooth. Hoping to overhear what they said next, I paused at the next empty table on the pretense of straightening the silverware.

"Don't you see how ironic that statement is, Melvin?" the woman said. "Thousands of women never even get a *chance* to see justice carried out against their attackers because you don't bother with processing evidence! Meanwhile, you put hundreds of quota arrests behind bars for random petty crimes and complain about how busy you are."

"Well, that's a very cynical way of looking at it," the sheriff replied in a flat tone that reminded me of a dentist I went to once. "We do our best."

"If you don't fix it, I go public," she said.

"Do you like beluga caviar, Calliope?" he asked. I rolled my eyes up at the clear blue sky. So that was the kind of business going down at Vista Mar. In the dining room, anyway.

When I went to the kitchen to get a couple of tourists their cold appetizers, the garde manger chef, a wiry, dark eyed woman about my age named Maria, shook her head as she cracked pepper over the top of a wedge salad.

"I don't know about all what's going on over here," she said, nodding her head over at Angelo, the head chef, a guy in his mid-thirties or early forties from New York with greased back hair and shifty eyes. I didn't like him much and had succeeded in staying out of his way thus far.

"What do you mean?" I asked, picking up the wedge and a chilled white gazpacho.

"You have to keep your eyes open with these machos," she said quietly, wrapping plastic over a clear container of sliced radishes, putting it back in the fridge under her station. "They try to get you to do their work for them. Me. You. Like we're their mom or something."

"What happened?"

"Pirate had you stock the bar and set up your tables today, right?"

"Yeah..."

"I prep my own station, all the vegetables, dressings, desserts, everything," she said, waving at the polycarbonate bins of neatly chopped herbs and bottles of dressings and sauces around her. She leaned toward me. "Today, Angelo had me prepping for the line too, because he came in late like Pirate. I don't know," she said. "Something's not right."

"How long have you worked here?"

"One month."

"Hmm," I said, "funny they were both late the same day."

"Sí?" Maria said, looking at me pointedly.

"I hear you," I said. "I'll... keep my eyes open."

We kept up a steady pace all evening. Later, after the sun went down, the outdoor heaters shed patchy warmth over a few tables of lingering outdoor diners. Calliope and Melvin had long since left. He had paid the bill, leaving exactly an 8 percent tip. She left two neatly folded twenties under her coffee cup. A match made in heaven. Weren't relationships all about balance? I tried to picture them going to a hotel together, having a torrid affair. I couldn't. Which was definitely for the best.

Nautical-style lamps around the edges of the patio cast shadows on the sand below the raised deck. I was waiting on two guys Pirate said were the CEO and CFO of an oil company, another table with a film producer and his much younger girlfriend or mistress, and an older couple on vacation from somewhere Midwestern. During a lull around nine o'clock or so, Connor (an avid surfer, as I discovered) and I were leaning against the bar, chatting about the local taco scene—slim pickings compared to what you find in East LA—when Wyatt emerged from his office. Rita trotted over to him, and they conferred in low voices. Connor and I stopped chatting, tried to look busy. I tried to hear what they were saying but couldn't make out the words over the forties jazz playing on the sound system.

"How old do you think Wyatt is?" I murmured to Connor out of the corner of my mouth as I filled ramekins with sugar packets from a little bucket on the shelf under the wait station. He shrugged. "No idea," he replied, smell-checking a pot of decaf to see if it had burned. "He's kind of . . . ageless, I guess." I watched as he went off to check on his customers. I didn't hear Wyatt come up behind me.

"My ears are burning," he said. I jumped.

"You scared me," I said, taking a step away, turning to face him. His eyes locked with mine and held them.

"Sorry," he said, winking.

I had no evidence of any crimes. I hadn't yet had a chance to ask him how he knew Gran. I wanted to know, badly. But if I asked him that, he might ask me how she was, and then I'd have to tell him she'd been murdered.

"Oh—I asked Connor if you're here every night. You know a place is good when the owner never leaves," I said, flattering him.

Wyatt nodded. He may not have believed me but seemed satisfied with my answer.

"Do me a favor, Queenie, bring me an Earl Grey with milk and two single malts for my friends out there on the patio." He pointed to the two men Pirate had identified as oil company execs. "Don't put them on the bill, of course."

"Sure thing," I said. "Not a drinker?"

"Not when I'm doing business," he said, "and it's all business to me. But you know that." He winked again. I bit my tongue to keep from asking him if he had something in his eye. Everybody has bad habits. It wouldn't do to get fired before I found another job.

"Coming right up," I said.

Eight

When I got home around midnight, I couldn't find my house key. I was always taking it off the ring so I didn't have to carry the whole bundle when I took Daisy out, regularly losing it in random sweatshirt and bag pockets. But I could have sworn it was on the ring when I'd left. At any rate, I was relieved to see a light still on in the kitchen. It was slowly sinking in that the house now belonged to me, but I wasn't quite ready to start thinking of it that way. Randy was waiting up for me, the crossword spread on the table, one of Gran's old black-and-white movies playing in the next room for company. "Where's my drink?" I asked, eyeing his tumbler of ice and amber liquid. "What is it?"

"Something I dug out of the back of the cabinet. Sweet. French. Not bad cold." He gestured to a dusty bottle on the counter. I kicked my work clogs off onto the mat inside the kitchen door and helped myself. The drink smelled of herbs and roots, reminiscent of the tinctures Gran made using this liqueur as a base. It brought her to me so strongly I just stood there, nose in the glass, blinking back tears. "Seven-letter word for snowbird or banner?" Randy offered, looking over his glasses at me. The hanging lamp, blue with orange flowers, cast a warm glow. Some vintage looking tarot cards fanned out before him.

"No idea," I said, dropping into the chair across from him. "I can count the number of times I've seen snow on one hand . . . These the cards Gran left Althea?" He nodded, gathering them into a pile and pushing the stack toward me.

"I had a look through the trunk, hope you don't mind me not waiting."

"No, I'm glad you did. I don't know how long it would have taken me to open it if you hadn't."

"There's a lot of her little books in there. Some of them look quite old. I'd say you're in for a wild ride," he said. Then he took a minuscule sip of his drink and leaned back in the chair, studying me with concern. "How's the head, niece? Intact?" I mimed patting the air around my head as if I'd misplaced it. He laughed. "Well, good you've still got your sense of humor, anyway. It'll get a fighter through anything." I rolled my eyes. "Seriously," he continued, leaning forward. "You're tough, you'll get through this." I worried the edge of one of the cards with my fingertip, willing my eyes to focus in on the image.

"Yeah."

"How was work?"

"Fine. Weird. I don't know."

"Mm-hmm." He skimmed a hand over the cards with a flourish as if he could divine the future just by touching them. If they had once been glossy, they weren't now. They were worn soft and papery, the color faded around the edges of some of them from being handled. "Pretty sure she painted them herself."

"They're beautiful," I said, picking up the top card. The Chariot. I fanned them out. The colors were faded but rich in tone. The texture of the paint made the images seem almost living. You could tell they'd once been vibrant. I'd come across a variety of tarot decks in new age bookshops and crystal stores around the city. This wasn't the traditional Rider-Waite deck, nor was it any deck I'd seen before. I'd even consulted a few psychics at different times in my life. Seemed to me there was a vast spectrum when it came to seers. Some were the real deal, and some were . . . not. Once, I agreed to see a psychic my college friend swore by who worked out of Coney Island and went by the name of Lady Fate. She wore full pancake makeup and a towering wig. Speaking through a fog of sickly incense, Lady Fate had told me I would one day discover I'm an impostor in my own life.

You'll see you're not who you thought you were, she'd said.

Sounds good to me, I'd replied. I never went back. I never owned a tarot deck myself or learned how to read them.

I picked up another. In fine black script, it read *The Star* along the bottom of an image of translucent moonlit evening glory vines twining around an arbor of bent willow branches, under which a brown-skinned woman with flowing dark hair and a midnight blue robe knelt, gazing into the reflection of the night sky in a dark pond. She had one hand outstretched, and the tips of her fingers grazed the surface of the water, sending ripples outward. A bullfrog watched from a nearby lily pad.

"Oils, I think," Randy mused. "She was talented."

I looked at the kitchen wall where a small, framed oil portrait hung. It was of Gran's dog before Daisy. The grass behind the shaggy dog showed many hues of sunlit green. The image showed exactly the goofy expression he had in life.

"She was," I said. "I can't believe she's gone. He shook his head, staring beyond me at one of Gran's old black-and-white thrillers, *Strangers on a Train*, on the boxy old television. "You didn't go for one of the comedies," I said, pointing to the stack of 80s movies beside the VCR that I had been watching to numb out each evening.

"Not in the mood to laugh," Randy replied, sighing. "Hey, if it's okay with you, I'm planning to take the sofa while I'm here . . . Can't imagine sleeping in her room just yet."

"Jesus, yeah, I understand," I said, feeling like the air was being squeezed out of my lungs again. It was becoming a familiar sensation. "I haven't been in there since . . ."

"You sure you're okay?" Randy asked, regarding me with concern. "You look mostly okay. A little tired." He managed a half-smile. "Not like you had a stroke or anything."

"Ha," I said. "I swear something strange did happen at the police station. It's—I was holding Gran's necklace."

"Of all of us, it'll be hardest for you," he said. "Seeing her every day, and now . . ."

"Yeah," I said. Tears pressed at the backs of my eyes. They were always there. I seemed to always be right on the verge of crying. "Her clothes . . ." I waved at the plastic bag I'd dropped next to my shoes by the door. I'd gingerly dropped the necklace back in the plastic baggie, careful not to touch the stone.

"Give it here," Randy said, beckoning for the bag of Gran's things. I passed it over. He formed the cards back into a pile and pushed them aside. "My letter said some of the same stuff yours did, about her childhood." He spread the top of the grocery bag open, reached inside, and drew out the baggie. The necklace looked awkward in there, like it didn't like being stuffed inside a cheap plastic Ziploc. He opened it, pinched the chain between fingertips, lifted it out.

"Hold out your hand."

I did. The pendant dropped into my palm. It didn't feel warm like it had at the police station. I examined the black stone. It was imperfect, rough. Not your usual jewelry stone. If it weren't for the gold setting it looked like it could have been picked up off a beach. I realized I'd never seen Gran without it, nor had I ever paid much attention to it before now.

"You should wear it," Randy said. "She'd want you to."

"How do you know?" I mumbled, still staring at the thing. I touched it with my fingertip and again had the sensation that it warmed at my touch. I looked up. The warm, buzzing sensation traveled up my arm. It was weird, but not unpleasant. Here, in the safety of home, despite what had happened to Gran in that very kitchen a few days earlier, the strange sensation was more comforting than frightening.

Randy shrugged. "I've just got a feeling about it."

"But what she wrote in the letter, about the camp . . . Losing her family . . ."

"I know," he said. "It must have been too painful to talk about."

I unclasped the necklace and hung it around my neck. He reached across and touched the stone.

"It doesn't feel warm to me."

"It must have been stress, like you said," I replied. "I'm imagining it."

"Well," Randy said, rising from the table with a soft groan, putting a hand to his lower back. "Memorial tomorrow. Time for this old man to get some shut-eye."

"Night," I said. I listened as he walked through the house to the bathroom, the click of the door. I let Daisy out in the backyard and put away the clean dishes from the dishwasher while waiting for her to do her business. Finally, I picked up the bag of Gran's things, locked the side door and back doors, checking them three times, and turned off the kitchen light. By the time I went through the living room, Randy was asleep on the velveteen couch with a throw neatly draped over him like a good soldier. I tiptoed through, Daisy on my heels, double-checking that the front door was bolted before switching off the small lamp on the desk. Tomorrow, after the memorial, I would explore the journals Gran had left me. Just had to get through it. After that, I hoped I'd have more energy to put into making decisions, like did I need a new job, and figuring out how I was going to afford to keep the house.

Before going to bed, I opened the door to Gran's bedroom, dropped the bag of her things inside, then shut the door quickly. It wasn't like I thought her ghost was lurking in her room. Even if it was, I'd never fear her presence, alive or dead. I was not afraid of some frustrated burglar or desperate addict. I *was* afraid of the glitch in the great universal plan that had allowed Anke Weiss Rivers to be murdered in her own home on a beautiful afternoon in May. I was angry at how she'd died. I just couldn't face her room, being surrounded by her personal things while the image of her body strewn on the floor kept flashing into my mind. It was too sad.

In my room, Daisy plopped down on the armchair by the window. She had claimed it as her official dog bed the night Gran died. I took a shower and put on pajamas. My body felt wired, and my mind buzzed with thoughts: the memorial the next day, work, cops, cops, and more cops. My poor brain didn't know where to land to even begin a normal anxiety spiral. I turned out the lights, lay in bed for five minutes, turned the bedside lamp back on. I stood and walked quietly out into the hall. Just enough light spilled from the open door of my room to navigate the living room where Uncle Randy was tucked up, snoring lightly. I went to the blue steamer trunk and felt around until I caught the edge of a small book. One of Gran's journals. Back in bed, I opened it. I touched the pendant around my neck. Time seemed to pause, the constant hum of the airport, sea, traffic, quieted. It read:

> *After we released from the displaced person camp I with several companions traveled by ship to the United States. For practice English I purchase this book. I was fortunate to learn English from my teachers in Foehrenwald. It was a long journey. Germany to Paris, then across the Atlantic to New York City, where a huge statue in the harbor of a woman holding a lamp welcome traveler. The ship was not clean. Comfort was minimal. Much illness. The journey was hard. But I am happy to be moving on. Europe is my past. America, my future.*
>
> *In New York, many of us boarded a train headed west. California. This is also a long journey. I am thankful that a few of the friends from the boat are still in my company. We shield each other from the men who do not have good intention feigning that we do not speak English and sometimes that we are ill.*
>
> *Now, I am in Los Angeles, living in the home of an older Jewish woman who has agreed to temporarily take in refugees from Europe. There are three of us girls. Each of us has a bed and some new clothes. I speak English so well, she says, that she would speak to a friend about getting a job for me at Union Station, the train depot downtown. She says if I am hired I will live in a house with other employees (they're called "Harvey Girls") and I'll earn a good wage. I am still always anxious and often can't sleep at night. Nightmares of Dachau haunt me. I'm better when I'm outdoors, and sometimes I go out at night and just walk and walk until I am so tired I can no longer stand up. But I feel fortunate to be alive and in a land with so much sun. And the sea.*

I put a marker in the journal, a nondescript little book bound in faded blue cloth with the word "diary" embossed in faded gold on the front, and the words *Anke Weiss, 1948,* printed neatly on the first page.

I thought of Gran arriving in LA, a stranger to this city so familiar to me, so much a part of my identity. She was right when she said young people didn't know how good they had it. My life had been a cakewalk compared to hers.

Nine

I was tired the next morning, as if my dreams had taken something out of me. The sound of someone in the yard beyond my window roused me from a deep, troubled sleep.

Foggy-headed, bleary-eyed, I lurched to my slightly open bedroom window and cranked it wide. Most of our windows didn't have screens as the sea breeze and arid climate mostly took care of bugs. I stuck my head out to see a young woman crouched by one of Gran's agave plants, apparently relieving herself.

"Hey!" I shouted, still groggy. Was I dreaming? The young woman was quite beautiful, with dark tangled hair to her waist and wide brown eyes. She looked as if she didn't get a shower often. Her clothes were worn and stained. A drifter, maybe, from one of the camps by marsh. The woman looked up, stood, pulling up her black leggings and releasing the hem of a tunic-like garment. She was in no hurry.

"Hey yourself," she said, seemingly unembarrassed to be caught in such a compromising position. "Is Anke around?"

I came fully awake.

"What?" I exclaimed, my mind racing. *How could she know Gran's name?* "Wait there," I said after a pause, my mind catching up, fitting pieces of the puzzle together. "Please, *please* don't go anywhere." What if this woman had something to do with the break-in, the attack? I frantically pulled on a cardigan. I glanced at the clock. Six twenty in the morning. Daisy, on the chair by my bed, lifted her head and yawned. "Don't you care there's an intruder on the property?" I hissed at her, shoving my phone in my back pocket. She stretched as if to say, *nope,* slid off the chair and followed me out of the room. Randy wasn't on the couch. His blanket and sheets were folded neatly and stacked on the ottoman. The bathroom door was closed, light seeping under the door, sound of the tap running. I walked quickly and quietly through to the laundry room adjoining the kitchen, out the door to the backyard, not bothering with shoes. Daisy ran out behind me, running over to her favorite spot near some long grass by the fence. I went directly to the side of the house, half expecting the woman to be gone. But she was there, perched on a lawn chair like any old guest. Daisy overtook me and bounded up to her. She leaned down to greet Daisy with equal enthusiasm.

"Daisy!" she said, as Daisy licked her hands and squeaked and squirmed with delight.

"It's been too long, my sweet thing." She looked up at me, smiling. Her voice was bright, clear, and just a little husky. She looked healthy, if a little pale (almost luminous?), right around my age. Did I know her? Was she from here?

"Sorry to alarm you," she said. "I didn't think anyone would be here but Anke." There was a ringing in my ears. For a moment, I couldn't hear anything, even though the woman was speaking and Daisy was still bounding joyfully around at our feet. The kids I'd grown up with in the neighborhood would have addressed Gran as Mrs. Rivers, not Anke.

"My grandmother . . ." I didn't know what to say. The woman stepped toward me, looking concerned. I must have looked fragile, because she took my arm and led me to the chair, indicating that I should sit. She smelled ginger-minty, like the yerba mansa root Gran harvested from the creek shallows to make a remedy for colds—before the creek got too polluted, that is. Mourning doves cooed the eaves of the house next door, songbirds twittering deep in the branches of Gran's massive toyon bush in the back corner of the yard. It was covered in white buds.

"How do you know my grandmother?" I asked, careful to keep my tone free of suspicion.

"Oh, I've known Anke for years," the woman said, pulling another chair over. "Sometimes she lets me stay here when I pass through."

"But *I've* lived here for years," I protested. "I mean, on and off, anyway. Except for college. And some other times."

"I know," the woman said. "It's true. We've never met . . . Anke spoke of you often." She looked up at the sky, which was blue and cloudless. "I visit when I visit."

Something about her vagueness and the fact that she seemed to feel totally comfortable using Gran's yard as a toilet suddenly filled me with resentment.

"Who are you?" I demanded.

"I'm Mo," she said. "Anke is my friend. I know who *you* are, Queenie. Just ask her."

"I can't," I snapped. "She's dead."

The woman's mouth dropped open. "Oh no," she said, shaking her head. "Oh no."

"She was attacked, right here in the house just three days ago. I took Daisy for a walk and when I came back—"

"You poor thing, I'm so, so sorry," Mo said, reaching out as if to touch the stone of Gran's necklace, still around my neck. I took a step back. "That's why you're wearing her stone," she murmured.

"She was *killed*," I spat through my tears, "by an intruder." I narrowed my eyes at her. "Was it you?"

She didn't answer, didn't look away, just held my gaze for a few tense moments. Finally: "No, of course it wasn't me." She looked away, then back at me. I believed her. Despite her strangeness, she seemed trustworthy. And Daisy, no fool when it came to character, knew her and liked her. "I'm truly sorry to bother you, this is a difficult time," she said. I hadn't noticed before, but her belongings were propped against the fence; some neatly folded blankets and a faded rucksack.

We sat in silence for a time, Mo stroking Daisy's ears and me taking deep breaths to calm myself. "I'll go," Mo said. "You must have a lot going on here."

"Where's home?" I asked when I felt in control again.

"I don't live anywhere," Mo said. "I travel."

"But how did you meet Gran?"

"It's a long story."

"I've got time."

Mo sat back and closed her eyes. "Anke and I met through mutual friends. She understands . . . sorry, understood, my lifestyle because . . ." She opened her eyes but with a soft focus, like she was examining something inside her own mind. She took a breath as if to reorganize her thoughts. "Anke, your grandmother, lived kind of like I do once. A long time ago. She was a wanderer too. For a short while."

I sat in the chair, planting both feet on the patchy grass. I rested my hands in my lap, looked at them. They were Gran's hands, but younger. Long fingers with knobby knuckles, tanned and strong. Working hands. Daisy, who had tired of the conversation long ago, was across the yard giving chase to some monarch butterflies who dared light on the purple flowering sage.

I shook my head. "I'm so lost," I said after a pause. "There was a lot my family and I never knew about Gran."

Mo nodded. "Yes, makes sense she would not have talked about it. But your grandfather knew her then."

"Did you know Grandad?—No," I shook my head again, "you couldn't have. You're too young."

Mo's face glowed with an inner mischief. "Appearances can be deceiving, Queenie," she said, reminding me of Gran. "I knew Cedric."

I took a deep breath. Waking up sounds drifted from the house. The tinny clanging of pots and pans passed through the open kitchen window and bounced off the backyard fence. The rich scent of fresh-brewed coffee. Randy was cooking breakfast, getting ready for the memorial. The yard needed to be set up, food prepared . . .

"Look," I said. "I'm feeling a little overwhelmed at the moment. Gran's memorial is today. You should stay."

"No, I should go before people get here," Mo said. She indicated her shabby clothes, her tangled hair. "I don't have other clothes."

"Come in and shower," I said, deciding to trust her. "I'll lend you some clothes."

"Okay," she said, after taking a moment to consider. "You're a good granddaughter, Queenie. She loved you very much."

Having put Gran through hell for years, I was well aware I could have been a better granddaughter. I should have been there when Gran was attacked. I'd failed her miserably.

"Come meet my Uncle Randy," I said.

By eleven o'clock the rented chairs were set up in the backyard, a few folding tables were ready to be covered in various cold salads; fruit, macaroni, three bean, potato, etc. Some of Gran's friends who I knew were sitting in pairs or small clusters. The younger friends, everyone below the age of seventy, seemed sad and subdued, while the ones closer to Gran's age spoke of her as if she were still alive, like they knew that they too would one day soon look down on plates of gluey macaroni salad being eaten in their honor. The fact that she'd died under violent circumstances cast an extra shadow over the whole thing, causing people to shift uncomfortably when a conversation drifted to the actual events around Gran's death.

"You found her, didn't you, love?" said a woman in her late seventies, shaking her head sympathetically like she knew what it was like to come home from an evening walk and find your grandmother dead. She lived next door in a house with a cactus garden out front. Gran had known her well, I think, but I didn't, and I resented her familiarity.

"Yes, I did," I replied, pasting on the expression I thought she wanted to see. Just then, Ben Schwartz, Gran's sort of hot lawyer, arrived holding the arm of an elderly woman with long white hair pinned up in a chignon, who

I assumed was his grandmother. He looked relaxed in dark linen trousers and a sky-blue shirt. "Excuse me," I said, "I need to say hello to a friend." Ben wasn't exactly a friend, but of all the guests, I was especially glad he was there. His grandmother greeted me warmly, clasping my hands in both of hers.

"I've long wanted to meet you," she said. "Your grandmother was a very dear friend. I just can't . . ." She shook her head, and I knew she was thinking about the attack, as I had many times since that night. Ben had probably shared with her at least the basic details. "I heard . . ." she started again.

"I know," I said, squeezing her hands. "It's been a shock. Thank you for coming today." I looked to Ben. "Both of you."

"Of course." She smiled sadly. "Of course, and we're here for you. Whatever you need—"

Just then, Manny walked into the yard, followed by Señora Chela. To my surprise, Mo ran up and embraced Chela. Daisy, who'd been napping in the shade, jumped up and ran to meet them, causing a bit of a commotion when she knocked over a chair holding a full plate in her enthusiasm.

"Hola, mija," Señora Chela said when they made their way over to me arm in arm. "I see you've already met my wayward niece here." Niece? Mo was Chela's niece? She squeezed my hand, and I mumbled something in response, too thrown to be coherent. "I'm so sorry for your loss. I knew your grandmother well, back in the day." Seemed like everyone did. Manny kissed my cheek and delivered his condolences as well. Then Uncle Randy was asking people to sit down. It was time to focus on remembering Gran. Excruciating as it was, I would need to wait to find out exactly how these peculiar new acquaintances of mine related to Gran.

Randy, calm and composed, gave a nice speech about Gran as a mother, role model, and confidant. A few of her close friends spoke, and my cousin Genevieve; Grandad's sister's daughter's daughter. She grew up nearby and she and I had been close as children. She'd adored Gran, called her Auntie, and had spent many days and nights at the house growing up. She'd gone to college up in northern California and stayed, but she said some words about how she and Auntie spoke on the phone regularly and that she didn't know what she would do without her. That made me cry to think about because I felt the same way, except probably even more so as I was used to seeing Gran every single day. And then it was my turn, and I got up in front of all those people, many of them total strangers, and tried to compress a lifetime of nurturance and unconditional love into a few sentences.

"My grandmother wasn't like anyone else I've ever known," I began reading from the notes I'd scrawled on my work notepad. "She was always there for me when it seemed no one else was . . ." After that, my vision blurred with tears, and I could no longer read from my notes. But everyone was staring at me intently, so I had to keep talking. I have no idea what I said, only that it didn't do Gran justice. When the babble of inadequate words stopped coming out of my mouth, I sat down in a chair as far from other people as I could get, feeling curiously emptied out. Ben brought me a glass of chilled lemonade.

After the talking was done, we put on music and brought out the food. I could hardly get a bite in for all the people who wanted to offer me their condolences, not that I had much of an appetite anyway. Mo, Manny, and Señora Chela helped with the food and clearing up, behaving more like family members than guests. My stomach was saying no to the potato salad. I had too much sadness and too many questions. I grabbed a paper napkin to wipe the mayo off my fingers and guzzled a glass of water. It was a hot day with very little breeze. I was sweating in my lightweight cotton sleeveless one-piece, and I'd developed a headache.

"Randy," I said, catching hold of his arm as he passed with a stack of dirty plates. "Let me take those." I took them and nodded to where Manny was helping the guys who'd come to pick up the chairs. "Recognize him?"

"Nope. Never seen him before today," he said.

"He knew Gran. And . . . Althea."

"Yeah?" he asked. "How?" I knew it upset him when Althea's name came up, that she wasn't at the memorial. She was his big sister. Gran was their mother. When Althea disappeared, I think he felt abandoned by her, too.

"Not sure," I said, setting off toward Manny. "Let's go find out." I stopped and half-turned. "Mo," I called. She had a tower of plates and cups balanced in her arms and the screen door propped open with one foot. She looked back.

"There are all these people, old friends of Gran. They're kind of strange." I spoke in an undertone so no one would overhear. "Manny," I called, waving him over. "You know my Uncle Randy, right?"

He came over, right hand outstretched, and clasped a surprised Randy's hand in both of his.

"Why, no," he said, all smiles and teeth. "We've never met. But I do know *of* you." The two men were exchanging pleasantries and I was working up the courage to ask Manny all the questions that had occurred to me after I'd driven away from his shop a few days before when we were interrupted.

"Excuse me," said a familiar, crisp voice. I turned. It took a second for me to place Detective Barnes without her trench coat. "Hello, Queenie," she said.

Her businesslike face was more mask-like than usual. "Sorry to do this now, but it couldn't wait. I need to talk with you right away." Her eyes flicked to Manny. I could almost see her scanning and cataloging all of our features, filing them away for later. "Is there somewhere we can speak privately, or do you want to come down to the station?"

"It really can't wait?" I asked.

"It's urgent," the detective said.

I hesitated. If I left the yard, I'd very likely miss my chance to grill Manny. But I couldn't say no.

"We can talk inside," I said, shooting an anxious look at Randy. Detective Barnes looked at him too.

"Are you Randall Rivers?" she asked. Randy nodded. "I'll need to speak with you after."

He nodded in baffled agreement, and I led the detective inside to the living room. She went to the window that looked out on the backyard.

"Do you want to sit?" she asked. It sounded more like a command than a question. I perched on the edge of the desk chair by the blue steamer trunk.

"You must have found something," I said. She turned her gaze from the scene in the yard to me.

"There's a witness."

"Who?"

"Someone passing by." Her tone was even, her cop's gaze sharply attuned to . . . me. "Well, there's more than one witness. That's why I'm here."

"That's good, right?" I asked, feeling inexplicably uneasy.

She did a slow shifting motion, side to side, as if to say it depends how you look at it. "Their stories don't match yours," she answered. "The accounts put you back here in the house at around the time your grandmother was assaulted."

Shock settled into my bones like water seeps through sand. "I—yes, that makes sense. I came home soon after it happened," I said. She held up her hand to stop me from speaking.

"You don't have to say anything without a lawyer present," she said.

"Why would I need a lawyer?" I asked. My voice sounded disembodied. I was floating, watching myself gripping the seat of the hard wooden chair with both hands.

"I'm sorry, Queenie," Detective Barnes said. She looked sorry, too. She looked like she was wishing she'd gone into another line of work. "You are a suspect in the investigation of Anke Rivers's death."

Ten

Did you see anyone on your walk? Was your dog leashed or unleashed? To the best of your ability, please recount your exact route and timing. Did you have any arguments or disagreements with your grandmother the day she died? Have you ever seen things that you weren't sure were real? Had intrusive thoughts? Had a psychological breakdown? Are you a drug user? How often do you drink alcohol and how much? How would you describe your mental state the evening of the incident?

During the questioning, something happened. Something so bizarre I've still never told anyone. See, I wasn't there on the sofa in Gran's house with Detective Barnes in a straight-backed chair opposite me, moving down the list of queries in her small red notebook. A brownish smudge on the back of the notebook by her thumb, coffee or maybe chocolate, was the last thing I noticed before I was lifted as if by a passing breeze. I saw my body, seated upright with both feet on the mustard carpet, hands folded in my lap. I saw Ben next to me (my body, anyway). Heard the first wave of questions and my calm answers. But I, the actual *me*, was above. I guess I just couldn't bear to hear more, so willed my non-corporeal self to rise, as in a dream. Up past the physical boundaries of the bungalow, high above the neighborhood, I rose to where I could see the sea. I stayed there for what seemed a long time, gazing out at the three-hundred-and-sixty-degree view. I looked down and saw myself sitting on the couch, calmly nodding my head, speaking with Detective Barnes. At the same time, it was like I could focus in on anything I wanted, no matter how far away, if I only thought of it. Vista Mar, a speck in the distance, rose before my eyes, every detail just as it was. I was a suspect in my beloved grandmother's murder case. I was being questioned as a suspect in a murder investigation. There was nothing to hold on to. Nothing but my job at Vista Mar. The only thing that could keep me afloat.

The rest of the afternoon passed in a stilted haze. Finally, awkward goodbyes. After the detective left, I sat for a long time, staring at the ashes in the hearth in the living room and thinking how my grandmother's beloved body had been reduced to just that. And did I kill her? Somehow? Without remembering? No! Absolutely not! But there had been the episode with Gran's pendant at the police station, where I drifted. And during the questioning. Was I losing my mind? Or had I already lost it?

Ben interrupted my mental spiral with a cup of herbal tea and a plate of chocolate chip cookies. "I'm not a criminal lawyer," Ben had said, sitting on the edge of the sofa a few feet away, elbows propped on his knees. "But I don't think this evidence will hold up. This is just how they do it, Queenie, they're required to follow up on every lead. No matter how improbable it seems or how painful it might be for the family."

"Okay," I said. My head felt so mixed up. It was nice he had faith in me. At that moment, I didn't. "Thanks for helping me today . . . I know you can't really be my lawyer, but I appreciate you standing in."

"You did well," he replied. "You answered all of the detective's questions very clearly. If you ask me, your alibi sounds solid. Now she'll be looking into the veracity of the witness and any motive that person might have to implicate you."

"So I'm not going to jail?"

"Not today," he said, taking a bite of one of the cookies.

"Why would anyone want to cast suspicion on *me*?" I asked.

Ben shrugged. "People do strange things," he said.

Indeed, they do. And they have strange experiences. Call them dreams or hallucinations . . . time lapses. I had not informed the detective about those. How could I?

Some mystery person, most likely a neighbor, had claimed to have seen me at the house at the time Gran was assaulted. I was ninety-nine percent positive that wasn't the case. Which meant one percent of me wasn't sure I could trust myself.

"Queenie," Ben said. He looked concerned.

I was breathing very fast. My hands were fluttering. I couldn't catch enough air to fill my lungs, which were spasming, and I could feel the rest of my body giving into a curious release of control. Then Mo was holding a paper bag over my mouth and nose. I felt a cool hand on the back of my neck. "Breathe," she was saying when the buzzing in my ears stopped, "you're going to be okay."

Randy came in and sat down across from me. "I have some hard news and some good news," Randy said. "I have to go back to San Diego tonight. Urgent business." I didn't say anything. Just looked at him. "Mo has agreed to stay with you for a few weeks," he continued.

I look up, taken aback. "Mo? But I only just met her."

"Do you have anyone else who could come stay? I don't want to leave you alone."

"Because you think I'm nuts?"

"No!" Randy exclaimed. "This situation is out of control, and you have every right to be overwhelmed. I just wish I could stay longer. What about friends?"

I put my head in my hands. "Everyone's so busy," I said. "They have jobs and ... lives." Translation: they are either bad influences or they want nothing to do with me.

"I'm sorry," Randy said, patting my knee. "I know. I understand."

"No, I'm sorry," I said, slumping back into the sofa cushions. I wrapped my arms around my face, squeezing my eyes tight to shut it all out. "What a mess."

"Mo says she's between jobs, just here visiting her aunt, and she'd be happy to help ... At least you wouldn't have to explain anything to her. She's already been filled in."

"True," I replied miserably. "Okay." I lifted my head to see Mo and Ben and Randy all exchanging concerned looks. "Okay! I understand I can't be trusted on my own." I turned to Mo. "I'm very grateful for the offer. If you don't mind the couch. I'm not ready to clear out Gran's room yet."

She nodded. "Of course," she said. "It's the least I can do. I can't imagine what you're going through."

Somehow, I felt she could. She was one of those people who seem to reflect back at you the parts of yourself you've been looking for but can't find. It was like, in her presence, I could imagine myself as someone good. Not now, but in the future. Maybe.

Later, after Randy and Ben left, I texted Arlo asking him to meet me. I threw the black dress I'd worn for the memorial in the back of the closet and put on clothes I found crumpled on my bedroom floor.

"I'm going out to meet a friend," I said to Mo. She was sitting on the couch reading a book from the shelf. She asked if I wanted her to come with me. Understandably, she looked worried about my leaving. I assured her I would be fine—I just needed to get out of the house—and walked down the street to catch the bus.

Detective Barnes's parting words echoed in my ears about not leaving the country and being careful what I said to people about the case. That they would be keeping an eye on me. While I kept an eye on Wyatt for Agents

Bresson and García, on Pirate and Angelo for Maria; the neighbors had their eyes on me too, and I needed to let off some steam. As I walked toward the bus stop, I looked around, wondering if people, police-people, were watching me, tracking my movements. It gave me a prickly feeling all over my scalp and down my back.

The restaurant portion of O'Malley's was dimly lit, quiet. Everyone was crowded around the bar TVs watching a soccer game. Buffalo wings and lager seemed to be the order of choice. I was early, and I didn't feel like waiting for him. I sat in the booth closest to the bathroom door and ordered steamed vegetables and a glass of white wine, hoping Arlo would understand I was there because I wanted the writing work he'd mentioned in his text, not because I wanted to be friends.

"Reginald!" he said, using my least favorite nickname. He leaned down, attempting a kiss on the lips, but I turned so it landed somewhere around my right ear. "It's so good to lay eyes on you." Right, that was why he'd visited me in the hospital once in the weeks I was there.

"Likewise," I choked out around a mouth full of overcooked broccoli.

"Can I get you another?"

"What?" I looked at my half-full glass. "Uh, okay."

He signaled the waitress, pointed to my glass, then sat down across from me.

"How've you been?"

"Fine," I said. "You?"

"Real good. *Real* good. How are you feeling? Wow, I haven't seen you since . . . the hospital," Arlo said, his hyped-up expression perhaps dimming just a bit at the memory. He unfolded his paper napkin like a man of the world, laying it neatly in his lap.

"I'm all right," I lied. "Got a new job." He flashed a smile in my direction, which accidentally hit the waitress, who was just dropping off my second glass of wine. Ping, like in Baywatch or something. She flashed white teeth right back at him. Arlo's hair was long enough to tuck behind his ears. His brown eyes were bright and energized. I could tell he'd been going to the gym.

"Me too!" he said, not bothering to ask about my job. He leaned over the table toward me. "Someone wants to make my show," he whispered conspiratorially, then he sat up straight and practically shouted it again, flinging his arms wide.

"Congratulations," I said dryly. Our lovely waitress gave me a dirty look as if to say *she* was happy for him, why wasn't I?

"What can I get you?" she asked, arching one penciled-in eyebrow.

"Steak and chips, please. And a beer." She offered him a drinks menu. He ran a finger down and stopped on one. "That's the winner," he said. I rolled my eyes. Arlo *would* consider a beer to be lucky to be drunk by him. And the attitude served him well. He took it with him into writers' rooms and emerged with connections and opportunities. And money. I was curious about what that felt like, to be handsomely compensated for doing work you loved.

"What's the word?" he asked, sitting back in the booth. "You good?"

I sighed and pushed my plate away. "Gran . . . died," I said, practically gagging on the words. The last thing I wanted to tell him was how bad things really were, how scared I was. How desperate. "Last week. Her memorial was today."

"Oh no. Shit. I'm so sorry," he said, reaching for my hand. "She was really old, but still, god, Queenie. Why didn't you say something? I would have come."

"I know. She wouldn't have wanted you there."

"Ouch," he said, not appearing in the least wounded. "Do you want to talk about it?"

"Not really," I said. "To be honest, I'd rather talk about anything else. Tell me about the show . . . you said . . . in your text a few days ago, that you might have some work for me."

It seemed Arlo couldn't get away from the subject of my dead grandmother quickly enough. Like, yes, let's change the subject. And the way he perked right up at my mention of the project made me feel like he really didn't give a shit Gran was gone. Granted, I hadn't told him she was murdered. But also, he hadn't even asked *how* she died. Wasn't that standard etiquette? I guess he'd always been an asshole. Somehow, it had never sunk in like it did now.

Arlo talked animatedly for a long time about a show for television he was developing with a buddy who was a producer.

He wanted my help.

He was going on about wanting to "utilize my vivid imagination," whatever that meant. I was trying not to think about Gran or Detective Barnes by gazing into my nearly empty glass and mentally willing him to order me another.

Then, for a moment, I allowed myself to vividly imagine a life spent writing. I imagined depositing Hollywood paychecks into my account, making homeowners insurance payments, and staying on top of bills without having to hustle . . . feeling secure. I imagined quitting the restaurant, how freeing that would feel. The thought of it allowed me to smile. It was a thin smile, but my spirits lifted, just a little.

I finished the second glass of wine. He signaled for another. The waitress seemed excited to have an excuse to come back to our table, dropping it within seconds of making eye contact with Arlo. So annoying.

A writing job. A real one. I couldn't believe it . . . That is, if I managed to stay out of prison. I pushed those thoughts down, hard. I hadn't done anything wrong.

"Sure," I said. "I'd love to contribute. What can you pay me? Enough to quit my current travesty of a restaurant job?"

His face clouded. "Sadly, no . . ." he said. "Not yet. I can pay you twenty bucks an hour out of my own pocket but it's not even close to full time." He shrugged. "It's still in development. Maybe when it goes to production?"

"Do I at least get a credit?" I asked. He nodded, reached for my hand again. "Yeah, yeah, of course you would. If it gets picked up, of course."

"I want it in writing," I said.

"Sure thing, sure thing." He dropped my hand and stood abruptly. I knew that detached, unfocused look in his eyes well. "Gonna hit the gents. Do you—?"

"No, I'm all set," I said, though the opposite was true. Part of me, the part I was trying to leave behind, would love a hit of something, but I wouldn't do that to Gran. Reaching over the table, I snagged a fry off Arlo's plate. It was limp, cold, and disappointing. But I needed more food in my belly to soak up the white wine, which wasn't agreeing with me. I felt woozy, chilly, and feverish at the same time. I wasn't sure I'd make it home on my own, and I was still spooked by the idea of people—cops, burglars—watching me, following me. It was late, and the last thing I wanted to do was walk through the dark streets of my neighborhood alone from the bus stop.

I stared out the window, waiting for the sky to lighten beyond Arlo's bedroom window while he snored beside me. It was a mistake to meet up with him at all, never mind go home with him, never mind sleep with him. But I was shaken to my core. I felt broken in a way I'd never experienced, even after the accident, and I craved a familiar presence. Uncle Randy had left, and Mo seemed kind, but she was a stranger. It just so happened that the most familiar person in my life who was still alive was someone Gran had warned me never to trust, someone I knew in my own heart was deeply untrustworthy. But some part of me needed to revisit who I had been before the accident, needed to hold her up for inspection and see what she was about; was afraid maybe that was the real me. It wasn't. Felt like stepping in fresh dog shit, but at least now I knew.

Eleven

I entered my kitchen early the next morning and hung my keys on the hook by the door. Mo was eating a single fried egg in the breakfast nook. "I was worried when you didn't come home last night," she said.

"Thanks for all your help yesterday," I said, avoiding her gaze.

"No trouble," she said.

I met her eyes and realized hers also had tears in them. Mine spilled over. "Sorry," I wept. "I'm hungover."

Mo swiped at the rivulets running down her cheeks and picked up the kettle to pour hot water over a filter of coffee grounds. She handed me the mug when it was ready. "Drink that," she said. "Go take care of yourself. Nap. Drink some water. Get yourself halfway human again. We can get to know each other later." She clapped her hands together. "How about I take Daisy for a walk? We can talk once you've rested."

"Okay," I said weakly, grabbing the coffee and sliding off the stool. I thanked her for the coffee and for taking care of Daisy. Did Daisy prefer her to me? Staring at my smudged, puffy face in the bathroom mirror while the water heated, I thought I wouldn't blame her.

The hot shower went a long way toward making me feel better. I knew I was innocent. Just because some neighbors saw me going into my own house didn't mean anything. They probably got the time of day mixed up.

Back in my room, clean and dry, I made the mistake of opening my laptop to check my email. There was a message waiting from Arlo: *The outline for episode 2 is attached. Work your magic,* it read. *This thing could really go places! Keep track of your hours and send me a bill at the end of the week. I'll give you cash. P.S. Nice to see you last night. Let's do it again soon.*

The sick feeling that had ebbed in the shower returned. Maybe it wasn't a white wine hangover after all, just the after-effects of Arlo's company. Good thing I was going into business with him (sarcasm implied). It wasn't Arlo's fault he was an ass, I reasoned. He'd been raised to think he deserved success, which wasn't a bad thing, necessarily. I shut the computer feeling a nauseating mixture of disgust and excitement.

"Queenie!" Mo called from the kitchen. "You okay?" I hurried to the kitchen, where she stood in the open door with Daisy still on the leash. The door was ajar. Pots and pans had been taken out of cabinets and strewn across the floor. Items on the counters had been moved around.

"I think someone's been in here while I was gone! Unless you did this?" Mo looked at me like maybe I had lost my mind. I shook my head. That this had happened while I was in the shower and I hadn't heard a thing was unnerving, to say the least. I shivered, wrapping my robe around myself more tightly.

"Should we call the police?" Mo wondered, peering around the door into the living room. The last thing I wanted was to talk to the police again.

"Let's see if anything's missing first."

On initial inspection, I didn't notice anything amiss, though now I could see whoever had entered had been in my room, and Gran's too. Dresser drawers had been opened and there was dirt in the carpet in the hallway that hadn't been there before. I returned to the living room, where Daisy was sniffing the carpet, excited by some unknown scent.

"Nothing's gone," I said, "just moved around."

Mo pointed to the blue trunk in the corner, the lid of which now lay open. "The lock's broken," she said.

I crossed the carpet in three steps, peered inside. It was empty.

None of Gran's papers or journals remained. "Holy shit," I exhaled, blinking as if that could make them reappear. It felt like a worse violation than a stranger entering my house while I showered, the theft of Gran's words, her memories. I rushed to my room, felt under the mattress where I'd tucked one of the journals—now the only one remaining. I breathed a sigh of relief finding it still there and hugged it to my chest, breathing hard. The pendant was where I'd shoved it in the pocket of my sweatshirt the night before. I put it on.

"No cops!" I shouted, shutting my door. "Just—give me a few minutes, I have to think." I threw myself down on my bed. Someone, Mo was the only one who could have, had changed the sheets. I buried my nose in the pillowcase breathing in the fresh scent of linen Gran had hung to dry out on the line before she . . .

My mind buzzed and gnawed with theories and worries. I closed my eyes, opened them, sat up. On the floor, I noticed the deck of hand-painted tarot cards had been knocked off my night table, likely by whoever had broken in. I didn't like seeing them on the floor, so made the monumental effort to lean down and retrieve them. I untied the ribbon and shuffled. A flat aged smell, not unpleasant, emanated from the worn cardstock. I didn't know much about reading cards, but I was curious. I thought maybe they'd offer me some encouragement. I cut the deck and turned over the top card. The Devil.

Hoping I might find something less ominous in Gran's journal, I propped up the pillows and leaned back, turning to the next entry in the one remaining journal. I didn't want to think about what had happened to the others. It was slim, the pages so thin they seemed like they might crumble between my fingertips. Her writing was neat and exact in her old-fashioned way. Her spelling and grammar were that of a non-native English speaker, still learning. German and what I assumed were Romani words and phrases were sprinkled throughout. None of the entries were dated or qualified. I would have to assume the writing was all recorded in 1948 or around there as listed on the first page of the diary. I turned to the second entry.

[Entry 2]
I got the job. Soon, I will be working at the lunch counter at Union Station. My interview was with a woman who asked many questions about my family and my "moral character and work ethic," as she put it. I was nervous because I did not fully understand everything she was saying about the contract and my responsibilities, but my hostess gave me a good reference and I have hope that it will all work out. Another girl in my house was also hired, and we will move together to a boarding house for Harvey employees. My hostess says the house has an impeccable reputation, and the restaurant too. The job is to make coffees and teas and plate meals, not to serve customers, but if I do well, I may soon be promoted.

There is more good news. Having kept the paper with the address of Sergeant Rivers's family home, I have been thinking ever since I arrived in California that I would try to find him and thank him for pulling me out from under the bed three years ago. But I have been afraid to do it. Getting the job at Union Station gave me the courage to ask my hostess for help with finding the address. Amazingly, it turned out to be not very far away. Last night, when I couldn't sleep, I walked to the house. It is a small blue bungalow with peeling paint and a beautiful garden of orange trees and bougainvillea. Maybe next week, once I've been paid, I will bake some bread and knock on the door.

[Entry 3]
Yesterday I took my first envelope of pay to the store and bought flour and soda and butter for whole meal buns, and a basket, and a new linen kitchen cloth. It is an incredible feeling to go to the store with money one has earned from working, to buy food and items to give as a gift. I have waited in countless lines for food served in the spirit of charity. Today, I bought and prepared food in the spirit of abundance and gratitude. This joy carried me all the way to Cedric Rivers's mother's house, where I

> knocked on the door, my legs shaking so I thought I might collapse if someone dared to open it. Then, there he was. He recognized me right away. He couldn't believe I was there, his eyes nearly popped out of his head. But he did seem very happy to see me. He introduced me to his mother and his sisters, and we sat on the front porch and ate the bread I'd brought and drank glasses of sweet, iced tea. I think tonight I will sleep peacefully for the first time in many, many years.

I'd heard bits of that story, how Gran and Grandad had met first in Europe during the war, and that they'd been reunited in the United States a few years later. He'd been one of the soldiers present at the liberation of Dachau. He'd helped her find a place at a temporary displaced persons camp. When she came to LA, she found him. The condition Gran must have been in when the soldiers finally showed up . . . I couldn't even begin to imagine. The pieces that had to fall into place for her to end up in LA; that by chance he happened to be at his mother's house on a short leave when she came looking for him. In 1948, he was still on active duty, stationed overseas. I remember when they told me the story, one night after dinner when we were all sitting out in the yard. I was learning about the liberation of the camps at school.

"Some people don't believe there were Black soldiers at Liberation," Grandad had said, shaking his head.

"Racist white supremacist people," Gran added.

"I was there," he continued, looking at her with such intense love in his eyes I remember I looked away. "That's when your grandmother and I first met."

By the next entry, Anke was promoted to serving at tables. I looked at my work-roughened hands, a constant reminder of her. It was comforting to learn that Gran had also labored in the hospitality industry, like me. I'd always thought of myself as the black sheep of the family. While you can acquire quite an education working in food service, you don't exactly get any framed certificates of accomplishment to hang on your wall. The new knowledge of Gran's past made me feel marginally less like a failure, and even proud of carrying on the tradition.

> [Entry 4]
> Today, I served coffee to a man who looked at me and remarked, "What a beautiful girl, you should be in pictures, you're that pretty." Then he looked me up and down as if his eyes could see through my dress. It seemed inappropriate, but it is also common. We are trained to be professional and polite. I said thank you and walked away. Later, he called me over again. He had been joined by another man, who he told me he is a producer in the films. He said the two of them

were talking and thought I would be just right to play a small role. He described the film as a Western, with cowboys and Indians. "You're just the right shade of brown," he said to me. "Not too Indian looking to play an Indian in the movies." I was confused because I've been learning that here in America, being brown-skinned and an immigrant means you are not welcome in many places. Cedric told me that people with darker skin often fear for their lives or miss out on jobs and opportunities because of how they look, that they're treated differently from other citizens, even in the army. The producer gave me a card with an address and a date and time scribbled on the back. He said show up and I would be on my way to becoming famous. I don't know about being famous, but I think I may go anyway. I understand that the Indians here are similar in some ways to the Roma. They have been persecuted, chased from their lands and killed just for being Indian. For this reason, I am interested in the role. The movie is based on a book, which I checked out of the library. In my nice uniform and with my employee identification card, they gave me a library card, even with my brown skin and my foreign accent.

I allowed the journal to drop in my lap. My eyes felt heavy, and I let them close. I was barely conscious of raising one hand to my chest to touch the black stone that hung around my neck. The blank darkness behind my eyelids wavered, then broke. Light streamed in. I thought of Anke as a twenty-year-old kid in LA. She'd lost everything, endured horrors I couldn't begin to imagine, yet she kept going. She was brave and smart and . . . against all odds, hopeful, despite everything she'd been through and the evil she'd witnessed.

I opened my eyes to a sunlit dirt street lined with weathered wooden shacks. It looked like an old Western town. There were men in old-fashioned clothes working cameras and booms. A guy in a light summer suit sat in a green director's chair, legs crossed. A lone woman stood by an open doorway. She wore a drab gray dress, her hair in two long dark braids. There was little sound but for hushed murmurings from people around me. Dust tickled my nostrils, making me sneeze. The air was dry, no wind. It smelled parched and sunbaked. I stood at the edge of the scene, completely unnoticed by anyone as far as I could tell. Then, the thundering of a horse's hooves on packed dirt. A man with long black hair rode up to the woman, pulled back on the reins hard, and dismounted. The cameramen moved to accommodate the shot. I squinted against the sunlight. The woman looked familiar. It was Gran, in full makeup and much, much younger than I ever knew her. The man handed her the reins, said something to her I couldn't make out. She replied, her words also indistinct, but the booms were right over their heads, capturing their exchange. I pinched myself hard on the arm, sure I was dreaming. It hurt. I looked down at myself, clad in a blue bathrobe, barefoot. Experimenting, I waved to a man with a pencil behind his ear who walked by me ten feet away. He paid no mind, didn't appear to see me at all. I stood there for what felt like a long time while they repeated the shot again and again. A woman in forties-era street clothes brought Anke water a few times, and another one touched up her makeup after wiping the perspiration from her forehead. The sun sank lower on the blue horizon. West was directly at the end of the street. The man in the chair called a wrap just as it reached the level of the buildings. The man with the horse handed it off to a groomsman, patted Anke on the shoulder in a congratulatory way, then turned and walked straight toward me. I watched him with curiosity. By his stature and good looks, I figured he must be the male lead. I gasped, feeling my mouth drop wide open. His hair was black instead of white, but there was no mistaking his identity. Walking toward me, sixty years ago on the set of my grandmother's Hollywood debut, was none other than Wyatt Jones.

I awoke in my bedroom gasping and drenched in sweat. I yanked my hand off the pendant resting on my chest and looked at it like it had burned me. Careful not to touch the stone, I undid the clasp and removed the necklace. I struggled to my feet. Holding it at arm's length, I kicked open my door.

"Mo!" I shouted, frantic. "Mo, help me!"

The back screen door slammed, and she came running into my bedroom. She took the necklace from me and placed it out of reach on my desk. Then I was sobbing in her arms. She guided me to the sofa chair, and we sat for a long time while I cried, and she patted my back soothingly. I was losing my mind.

Mo shook her head. "You are going to be okay, Queenie," she said.

"How do you know?" I was totally spinning out.

"I know more than you realize," she said. "I'm here to look out for you, okay? We weren't sure if this whole thing would get out of hand enough to have to intervene, but it seems like it has."

"This whole thing? Who's we?" I asked, pulling away from her.

"Your grandmother wasn't who you think she was, and neither am I," she said, glancing at the pendant. "And neither are you."

Twelve

The land is a sentient being, Mo said. It has always selected certain humans to act on its behalf. In the past, these people were revered as deities. Mythologies and entire systems of belief and ritual were created around their powers. Do you really believe that once there were gods, but they all disappeared? Or that the old stories were fabrications? There are thousands of us, growing in numbers every day.
We're still here.
Some of us act consciously, we know what and who we are.
Some don't know who they are, but by being in the world and of it, they influence the ebb and flow of existence.

Mo, are saying you have magic powers? That Gran did? That I do?

Yes and no. I can't snap my fingers to make something happen. But I can feel into something, listen to it, and help guide it in the right direction.

And the others?

Yes.

Q, Manny, and Señora Chela?

And Wyatt, Rita, Shen, Pirate. All of us. Many years ago, there was a rift. Wyatt and Q fought. They went one direction, and the rest of us went another.

Oh. So you all know each other. And Gran was . . .

One of us.

Tell me, if you all have powers, why is the world such a mess?

Some beings influence for the good of all. Some don't.

Okay.

Do you believe me?

No.

Mo rose from the couch, walked to the center of the room. She seemed to glow, illuminated from within. I can look back on this now and it makes sense because I know her, but at the time, I was reeling. Like a full moon, silvery light emanated from her, extending an aura that unfurled into every corner of the room, enveloping everything, including me.

You know when you go out at night and the moon is so big and so there, it bathes you in a special peace like nothing else? When your thoughts are dull, and the moon sings them into meaning.

I realized that throughout our very bizarre conversation, Mo hadn't spoken aloud. Nor had I. Rather, I heard her voice in my head, and somehow projected my thoughts into hers.

Anke's talent was accessing the thin places of time and space, Mo said (thought). Her pendant is an ancient piece of basalt from a special place, a charmstone that allowed her to time travel. When she died, she passed on her abilities to you, through the stone.

But if you all have powers, why couldn't you protect her? Why couldn't she protect herself? (Why, why, why?)

We do have powers, but they're limited. Especially when we're separated. Together, we're stronger. But we've been splintered for a long time. It's been hard. Q and Wyatt can't be in the same room without trying to kill each other. The rest of us have been forced to choose sides.

See, it all began before my time when Wyatt participated in the 1785 rebellion against the Mission San Gabriel. Q wanted to wait, build the resistance over time. Wyatt disagreed. When Anke came around, she got to know Wyatt first. Then she met Q and he—their feud, the way they try to manipulate all of us and undermine each other—it drove Anke crazy. After she married Cedric, she got really good at boundaries. Just didn't want to be involved. Didn't want her family to be affected.

Q—Quaoar—has always been here, forever. Thousands of years. Wyatt—Weywot—is his son. Chela, Pirate, Shen, Rita, Manny, and I are much younger. One might even say we're new to this place; foreigners who have made it our home.

Pirate was chosen by the land sometime around when Pueblo de Los Ángeles was established in 1781. He was one of the twenty-six founding residents of African descent.

Chela really is my aunt. We're from what is now called Mexico; we're Mestizo, of mixed Native and Spanish descent. We came here in 1912, during the revolution, after my parents were killed in the fighting.
Rita's family were English and Scottish, I think. They crossed the country from the East Coast in a covered wagon in the 1840s.
Manny and Shen originally came from China. They both went to northern California as laborers during the gold rush, then moved down here in the late 1800s.
Anke was just a baby compared to the rest of us. As you know, she came to Los Angeles after her family were all killed in the Holocaust.
Q weaves the net of all creation, tends the flow of existence. Wyatt knows the sky. Pirate, the sea. Chela listens to the earth. Manny talks to plants and trees. In China, he learned herbal medicine from his grandfather, who was a healer. Shen resonates with the metals that emerge from the earth. That is, of course, why he's so good at wealth management.
Rita is Coyote, a trickster.
I am the Moon. Yes, there are other moon-guardians. I'm not the only one. And there are sun-people. And wind-people . . . None of us are particularly special. We're just . . .

Paying attention, I thought.
Yes! Mo answered. That's it. We pay extra attention; we listen and feel what's going on around us. Through doing so, we develop certain skills and abilities.
Anke was a guardian of the subconscious. Of time and space, memories, dreams, and visions. Now, you are.
I spoke aloud: "Are you saying . . . I could go back in time and find out what happened to Gran, clear my name, and maybe stop her from being killed?" *My words seemed to shatter the glow that had infused the room. A shadow passed over Mo's face.*
Mo gave me a look. "Time traveling poses enormous risks, consequences you couldn't even begin to comprehend," *she said. I gazed back at her, feeling utterly helpless. I believed her. Or part of me did. The other part was still catching up. How could she stand there and tell me I had the power to go back in time, that it was possible for me to change the course of events that led to Gran's death, but that I couldn't?* "Everyone knows you can't meddle with time!" *Mo said.* "Playing God always has terrible consequences."
She said it was time to go to Manny's, that it was all too much for her to handle on her own, and that they might be able to answer the questions she couldn't.

When we left the house about an hour later, the air had turned thick and dusty, more so than on a typical smoggy day. It smelled like burning. "Wildfires," I said. I turned left at the end of the street, climbing a winding hill up to a stretch of road overlooking the bay. I pulled over onto the narrow shoulder and peered through the windshield out to sea. Due south, the faint outline of Catalina was obscured by a dense haze of fog and smoke. A plume coiled energetically out of the fog, sulfuric yellow dragon's breath. It fanned out over the water in a curving pattern, pushed northward by the swirling counterclockwise eddy.

I got out of the car and walked to the guardrail. Below me, cars sped along a roadway that hugged the coast. Looking north and inland, the bowl of a city gathered smoke and mist from the sea into its greedy belly, the hills and mountains encircling the city, a ring of ancient sentries. For hundreds of years, those mountains kept European invaders out, but eventually, inevitably? Their defenses failed. Come evening, the wind would likely change. The dirty air would flow seaward. I got back in the car and put up the windows before remembering the AC was broken. "Which is worse?" I asked. "Smoke inhalation or dying of heat?" The overall effect of smoke and fog and sun created a feverish atmosphere of murky gray-gold. Mo coughed and shrugged.

When we arrived at Manny's, he had one of the café chairs out on the sidewalk. There he was, sitting with legs crossed, as if waiting for us. Some of the coincidences and synchronicities I'd experienced, not only since meeting Gran's old friends, but throughout my life, were starting to make sense. It was like picking out a pattern in something that at first appears random.

I parked in the lot in front of the store. Señora Chela's roasted corn and butter aromas wafted in the open windows. The smoke smell was less oppressive in this part of town, or maybe the winds had shifted slightly. I found that I was looking forward to going into the cool, dim interior of Manny's. Specifically, I wanted to talk to Q.

Manny greeted us in his offhand way. "Shall we?" he said, rising to hold the door open. We walked without speaking single file through the empty store. Manny led the way to Q's room. The door was ajar. A triangle of light spilled into the hall. A humming sound emitted from inside. Manny let me pass. I stepped closer, peered inside. A gravelly rising and falling hum emitted from deep in Q's throat. It was prayers in a monastery on a misty mountaintop with rain dripping from stone gutters. It was summer mornings with nothing to do but read. It was Gran brushing my damp hair a little too hard on a rare, stormy evening while thunder rumbled and shook the foundations of our little bungalow. *I hate my freckles. A boy at school tried to count them today. Ouch.*

Like stars. Your freckles remind him of the sky at night. If I don't brush the tangles out, we'll have to cut them.
   Rosa says they look like chocolate polka dots.
   What do you like better, sweetheart, chocolate or vanilla?
   "Chocolate," I whispered to myself, to Gran many years ago. Tears rose behind my eyes. I was sick of crying, so I forced them back. Q ceased humming but did not acknowledge our entrance otherwise. Mo entered the room behind me. I went with her, sat on a three-legged stool near Q. We were surrounded by yards and yards of tan-colored netting smelling of dried plant matter and complex ancient resins like spikenard and frankincense. As my fingertips grazed the tightly spun fibers I heard voices, breathing, sounds, wind, and I was spinning in a field of shifting light and dark. I took my hand back quickly. Q was watching me. He nodded, smiling.
   "What is it?" I asked.
   "Oh—everything," he said, not pausing in his work. His compact sturdy fingers wound lengths of twine into each other like magic; I could see no knot, and yet he bound them effortlessly, then turned it over quickly this way and that and another diamond-pattern segment was complete. "Some call it Creation. Others, art. Still others, a fishing net."
   I sat carefully on a stool. My breathing became easier, and my mind felt just a little bit clearer.
   My gut said to trust them, to take the leap. What choice did I have? One half of me believed and was ready to live in this new world in which there existed beings with special abilities and responsibilities. The other half was scared, skeptical, and wanted to get up and walk out. I really didn't know.
   I resisted the urge to touch Anke's pendant around my neck. My . . . inheritance.
   "You have taken a shine to Mo, anyway. I can tell," Q said, as if reading my mind. Perhaps he was. He laughed at his pun, a deep belly laugh that caused the net to shiver, rippling waves in all directions. A rumbling in the ground beneath us mimicked the gentle rolling motion of the net. We all went still. It went on for a few seconds, then Señora Chela popped her head in the door.
   "Calmate, Q," she said, "the land is tender today from the wildfires and I can't bear the shaking." Then she noticed me. "Ah, Queenie. I forgot you were coming today . . ." She looked at Manny as if to ask, *does she know?* Meanwhile, I was wondering how she knew I was coming to visit that day . . .
   Quaoar, creator. Chehooit, Quaoar's partner, guardian of earth and harvest. Moar, the moon. Weywot, the fallen son, guardian of the skies. The

words and rhythms of the Tongva and Chumash stories Gran used to tell me on our walks came back in pieces. Tukupar Itar, the trickster. Pamit, guardian of the sea. I remembered them all. Was it possible the . . . gods . . . were not myths but real flesh and blood . . . also changed but still here?

Or had I made this all up? Was it possible I was constructing an alternate reality for myself out of details from those memories of the stories Gran used to tell? Some sort of projection, a . . . trauma response.

"I had a weird dream today," I said shakily. "Gran was on a 1940s film set. She was an actress. I saw . . . my boss, Wyatt Jones."

There was a stretch of silence, during which I became keenly aware of the low buzz of all the light fixtures in the room, the heat they emitted.

"The past can shed light on the present," Manny said. He'd been leaning against the wall by the door, quiet until now.

"Sure," I agreed.

"But sometimes, when you dig up the past, you learn things you'd rather not have known." His words echoed what Mo had said earlier. "Are you sure you want to learn about the past?"

"Yes," I said. I wasn't sure.

"I first met Anke Weiss outside Central Library, downtown, where she was scraping together enough money for food and not much else, reading tarot cards," Manny went on.

"I thought she worked at the café at Union Station?"

"She did. But she was fired once she started showing." He gave me a meaningful look.

"She was . . . *pregnant*?"

Manny nodded.

"She wasn't married to Grandad yet?"

Manny shook his head. "She had, in fact, found Cedric Rivers in LA using his mother's address, but in '47 a former army chaplain recruited a number of Black soldiers to an organizing committee working to desegregate the military."

"Including Grandad?" I asked.

"Yes," he said. "Cedric Rivers was involved with the effort, covertly, of course, because he was still in active service. When that fellow, Randolph I think his name was, testified before the Armed Services Committee in DC in March of 1948, he threatened that the league would urge African Americans to refuse to serve in the military—until they could serve as equals. Rivers was one of their inside men. As I understand it, he helped organize within the army to ensure that if the government didn't take Randolph seriously, that there would be a sudden mass exodus of service-people. With the Cold War and Korea looming on the horizon, the US could ill afford to lose so many enlisted bodies, never mind the ones who would choose not to enlist if there was a boycott."

"Wasn't that a dangerous position for him to be in?" I thought of my Grandad, always so steady and kind. People loved him. They would have listened to him.

"Very," Manny replied. "And busy, too. I understand he and Anke got in touch shortly after she arrived in California, but he wasn't around much for a while there."

"So, Mom was conceived out of wedlock... Grandad's mom wouldn't have approved," I said. "Great-Grandmother Rivers, worried about the kind of life her son was choosing with someone she considered to be an outsider, gave Anke a hard time for years, until she was eventually won over."

"Rivers didn't know Anke was pregnant, jobless, and homeless. If he had, being the type of man he was, he would have done something, helped her somehow... even though the child wasn't his." Manny's green and violet eyes appeared to turn a deeper, forest hue, and the slender purple rings around the iris stood out in contrast. They reminded me of datura, a nightshade also known as toloache and jimsonweed. It was a plant that grew abundantly on the bluffs. Big, trumpet-shaped blooms fading from lavender to white that emerged out of a tangle of fuzzy green leaves. Poisonous if too much is ingested. Gran had loved to catch them half open. Sometimes we stood for a long time, trying to detect the infinitesimally slow movement of the petals as they opened or closed.

Even though the child wasn't his. Those words drifted in one of my ears and out the other, I couldn't grab onto them.

"I met Anke Weiss soon after she was let go from her job at Union Station," continued Manny. He shook his head. "Harvey girls weren't allowed to get pregnant and continue working."

"I'm confused," I said. "How did she get pregnant?" *Even though the child wasn't his.* "I thought Grandad was stationed overseas at the time?"

"She met Wyatt Jones on the film set. He was the lead. She had a small part." I was feeling very cold suddenly despite the warm room. My hands and feet tingled. A roaring in my ears caused me to miss Manny's next words. I had to work hard to make my mouth form words.

"Repeat that?"

"It wasn't your dream you saw," Mo said gently. "It was Anke's real life. In the past. In 1948. Wyatt Jones went by the name of Whittier Clark back then . . . He tried his hand at acting for a while . . . Didn't really work out. That film never even made it to the screen, things fell apart before they even finished shooting. Money problems or something. Anyway, as I understand it, one day Whittier Clark flew into a rage on set, something one of the film crew said to him, I'm not sure. He attacked the guy. Anyway, Anke stepped in and talked him down. As I understand it, they became friends, and . . . had an affair."

I didn't know what to say. "You mean I'm not . . . Grandad? Mom is . . ."

Q lifted his eyes from his work. "We don't know for sure what happened. Wyatt and Anke refused to speak about it."

The implications of it crashed in on me all at once, but one thing stood out: If it were true, I was not my grandfather's blood relative. It meant I wasn't Black, I wasn't his granddaughter; that a piece of my identity, so crucial to how I saw myself, had been a lie all along. It meant I was . . . Wyatt's granddaughter.

"Cedric Rivers was your grandad," Q said, again, as if reading my mind. "He took Althea as his own child. But, yes, it's likely you and your mom are not his biological descendants." *Likely.* Q said likely, not certain, which meant there was room for error, room for them to be wrong. He fiddled with a fold of fishing net. "I imagine Anke never told you as a way of protecting you and your mom."

As a way of protecting us . . . from what? From . . . Wyatt? If that was the case, why had Gran sent me to work for him right before she died?

"To protect your family's reputation. Back then, a child born out of wedlock would not have been considered legitimate." Ha, I'd been born out of wedlock, too.

Someday you'll find you aren't who you thought you were.

Lady Fate's Coney Island prediction. I had thought it a farce and her a fake at the time, but maybe there was something to Lady Fate after all.

I imagined Gran as a young woman. She'd spent much of her adolescence imprisoned in a Nazi camp. Newly arrived, how would she have perceived America? Even back then, maybe the American Dream probably didn't strike her as quite so dreamy after all once she was here. Or maybe it did. She and Grandad had found each other, after all. She had seemed happy when I was growing up. In America, I was aware, Roma people were often perceived as dishonest, even criminal, especially by the police. In 1948, Gran's circumstances had improved since Dachau, but not much. It was no wonder she'd kept so much of her identity and her past hidden. Gran always said I had Grandad's eyes. What could she have *meant*, saying such a thing, if she knew it wasn't so?

There was always a part of her that seemed closed off. Now I had some idea of why she might have needed to hold a part of herself back from us—some damaged part she didn't want to touch us. That I could personally understand.

I thought of the trunk, always locked, that contained her secrets.

"Isn't Wyatt . . . trustworthy?" I asked.

"My son was given too much power too soon," Q said. "It corrupted him. He became greedy and entitled, no different from a child who is handed everything and never disciplined or taught to care for others. He presumed that the world was an extension of himself, existing to manipulate as he sees fit. We believe my son is becoming so obsessed with materialism, he will soon be fully integrated into the world of money and power . . . lost to us forever."

"My visions," I began, running a section of the net through my hands, "you say I can go back in time, but I shouldn't. I . . . need to find out who killed Gran and—"

"You have to promise you won't time travel," Manny broke in. "It's far too dangerous. The vision you had earlier was a projection of your mental sphere through time. Because you held the journal, you were able to enter a dream that was somehow linked to the journal."

"But I could just go back to the time of the murder—"

"No!" Q jerked his head up to look at me. The earth below us gave a warning rumble. Señora Chela shot him a look. "No," he said more calmly. "To dream-travel is one thing. To *time* travel is quite another."

"Is it dangerous to dream-travel, like I did earlier?"

"Dream-travel is . . . unpredictable," Q said. "But dangerous only in the sense that you might see things you would have been better off not seeing." He looked pointedly at me. "You can't decide what dream you see . . . The dream chooses the traveler, not the other way around."

The dream chooses the traveler. I've always felt the pull of the supernatural. Raised by Gran, I was raised believing in a sort of nebulous, world-permeating nature-magic. But this was all too much. Just, too much. Unable to fully digest everything, I fixated on one thing, just one thing I might be able to do myself: I had to find out who killed Gran.

Whoever had accused me of being home at the bungalow when Gran was attacked could also give me information about what had actually happened. And the reason they had lied would provide a clue.

Thirteen

That afternoon, Mo and I ordered pizza, drank lemonade, and watched a romantic comedy in which two people meet, hate each other, realize they actually like each other, get confused, then fall in love. If only life were that simple. We didn't talk about what had been discussed at Manny's. A couple of hours before sunset, I felt calm enough to go in search of the witnesses. Mo wanted to come with me, but I refused. "Too distracting," I told her.

"Just be careful," she called after me.

See, I remembered the new neighbor in the suit from the day in question, how he'd noticed me walking by when he got out of his car. It had seemed an appraising glance, appreciative, like maybe he found me attractive. I wondered if I might be able to glean some information from him by capitalizing on that. I could ask him to vouch for my alibi.

I never really thought I was in danger of being held responsible for my grandmother's death. My status as a suspect was inconvenient—a nuisance and an insult. It added to my overwhelming sense of guilt and made me feel vulnerable to a myriad of external forces: police investigators, the real murderer, the justice system. I had no criminal record (a miracle, but true). Everyone knew what a good relationship Gran and I had. But it was destabilizing, shameful to have been accused in the first place, stressful to be put through police procedurals when I was grieving an absolutely gutting loss. I had to find a way to clear my name. But to do that I had to stop feeling like a victim and pull myself together. Also, I was angry. Whoever had done this needed to be held accountable.

The first neighbor I visited was the lady next door. Her cactus garden consisted of clumps and mounds of furry little protrusions, some with pink, orange, or yellow blooms, interspersed with big green ball-shaped cacti covered in yellow spikes. Two magnificent prickly pears boasting ripe fuchsia fruit were at the center of each sandy patch on either side of the walk, holding court for the smaller specimens. She answered the door wearing an apron printed with yellow ducks on a blue background. The thick aroma of something baking hit me when the door opened, a sweet wall of scent.

"Hello, dear," cactus lady greeted me. I'd known her name once but had forgotten it. She smiled, but it didn't reach her eyes. "How are you holding up?"

"Oh, fine, thanks," I said, conscious of standing with my shoulders back, arms loose like a person who has nothing to hide. "Sorry to bother you. Wow, that smells delicious." It smelled overly sweet and slightly synthetic. Like blueberry muffins, you buy in a package at the airport.

"Cake. Not ready for some time. Otherwise, I'd offer you some."

"Right," I said. "No trouble . . ."

"Oh, I can drop some over later, maybe," she said, a little anxiously, it seemed.

"Really, it's okay. I just wanted to quickly ask you a question if you have a sec?"

She glanced behind her as if hoping for a distraction. Nothing appeared. "I have a moment before I need to check the oven."

"I'll be fast," I said. At this point, I was wondering why she didn't just invite me in. "There were some . . . people who say they saw me at home when Gran was . . . assaulted." I had to take a breath to steady my voice. "I—don't know why that would be because I was out with Daisy at the time. Did you happen to notice anything that day? From your window?"

"Oh my!" she said, appearing appropriately shocked. But did a shadow of fear pass across her face before she spoke? "That's just terrible. I didn't see anything at all! Crikey, the cake is burning. Queenie, I can't really talk now!" She was waving her dish towel in the air and a sheen of perspiration had broken out visibly on her forehead. "Sorry to say I was not home that day and cannot help you."

"But you were home," I said. "I saw you . . . remember?"

"Oh! Um, please do—" At this, she broke off, seemingly unable to form another excuse. She stared at me in a state of pure panic for a beat before taking two steps backward and slamming the door in my face.

And that was how I figured out who the "snitch" (probably) was. I should have known. Cactus garden lady was always peering out her windows from behind her lace curtains.

Next, I went down the street to hopefully obtain my alibi for Detective Barnes.

The black sedan was in the drive as I knew it would be since it was past six. I combed my fingers through my wavy hair that Gran always called honey-brown and I called mouse brown. I suppose in the summer months I do get some nice highlights. In preparation for this task, I'd applied olive-toned tinted moisturizer to my olive skin, which made exactly no difference to how my face looked. I'd also put on some lipstick and mascara and my favorite tight black jeans with a white t-shirt that showed some cleavage. So, feeling like a regular Lara Croft with wavy honey-brown hair, I strode up Mr. Regular's walk, hoping my assessment had been correct and that he didn't have a wife.

"May I . . . help you?" he asked, answering after the seventh doorbell ring with a glass of what looked like whiskey and rocks in one hand. Lucky me.

"Oh, hello."

"You're . . ."

"A neighbor. I live up the street. Right over there." I pointed to the top of the curve in the hill where the pink bungalow shone in the almost set sun.

"I'm Damien," he said.

"Queenie." I put out my hand to shake and gave him a good one, just like Grandad taught me. Firm and no-nonsense. See, even when you want to attract flies with honey, you've got to make them think you are a boss. Because most men like a challenge, and if you are a boss the man thinks he might eventually be able to control, he will engage until he meets that goal. Only a man who can subdue a boss is a real man. It is a rite of passage. In many circles, this is how it goes. I don't make the rules. I've just learned them through years of experience. You don't make a living serving food and drinks by being dumb. A lot of people think so, but it takes balls and brains to make it in hospitality. You are always juggling—not just plates, but egos.

"Hi, Damien. I—see, I know this maybe sounds strange, but the other day I was walking past and . . . we waved to each other? Or, rather, I waved, and you sort of nodded."

He looked confused and shook his head, but asked, "Do you want to come in? It's so cold out here. And I don't have a wife."

"You don't have a *wife*?"

"A *life*. I don't have a life is what I said."

"Ah," I faked a laugh. "Sure, um. Okay? I just have a question. Shouldn't take long."

"I don't have a wife either," he clarified, smiling. "What I was trying to say was that I work all the time and I don't have a life outside of it. I would be grateful for some company."

"Sure," I said, stepping over the threshold that looked like a piece of mahogany cut from the rainforest, "let's chat."

The open-plan kitchen and living room were brightly lit, fitted with stainless steel appliances and granite countertops, white walls. Large and minimally furnished, the house didn't feel lived in. All the windows and shades were shut tight. The only discernible smell was of lingering polyurethane, which I assumed was from the highly polished almost sticky-looking wood floors. Damien offered me a drink, which I accepted. Burying my nose in the tumbler of scotch created a smoke and varnish blend that made my head spin before I'd even had a sip.

"So, you moved in . . . ?"

"A month ago," he said, corking the bottle and setting it on the counter. "I just moved here for work. From Portland. Consulting."

"Huh," I said, feigning interest. Damien gestured to a swivel stool at the counter, but I didn't want to sit. Somehow, it seemed like to do so would be strategically weak. I had a task to accomplish, and I had promised Mo I'd be home in time for dinner. "What kind of consulting?"

"Oh, you know. Corporate this and that. The house is owned by my employer. What do you do?"

Instead of answering, I wandered the space, taking a theatrical taste of my drink while pretending to examine the large flat-screen television attached to one wall. The liquor burned my throat and made my eyes water. An unpleasant warmth radiated across my chest and belly, accompanied by a restlessness in my limbs. Despite the size of the room, it seemed, suddenly, like the walls were closing in. I was dying for some fresh air. I appreciate a good whiskey and a nice man in a suit, but something felt . . . not right. Damien's eyes tracked me as I moved around the room. He was still waiting for me to answer his question as I circled back to the kitchen island. "I'm a—I work at a restaurant. For now. But writing is my real interest. I never finished college. And I've felt sort of lost ever since."

He nodded along while I rambled, as if what I was saying was the most fascinating thing in the world. "I hear behind-the-scenes restaurant culture is wild around here," he said. "Drugs and late nights." That was when I noticed he wasn't drinking. His glass had been full when he answered the door, and it still was. "So, you like to party?" Damien said a little too eagerly. "I've got some molly upstairs . . ."

"No!" I burst out, having apparently lost control of my volume. *Oh, mister. If you only knew how much I'd like to meet your friend Molly.* I misjudged the distance from my hand to the counter accidentally slamming the glass down on the counter. I took a deep breath of the stifling air, trying to clear my head. "I don't use. Anymore. Not since I was in a bad accident . . ."

"Ah, okay," he said. "Yeah, it's not mine. Someone at work gave it to me." He reached out and patted the hand that gripped the counter beside the brown puddle of whiskey I'd spilled. "Sorry to hear about your accident."

"Mm-hmm, thanks."

"Anyway, what can I do for you? Out front you said you had a question."

Oh, thank god. I could ask the damn question and get out. In my opinion, small talk is a treacherous landscape disguised as a walk in the park. One second there's soft green grass beneath your feet, the next you've been sucked into a black hole of microaggressions and misunderstandings you can't refute because . . . it's just harmless chitchat, right? I closed my eyes briefly in an attempt to reclaim my train of thought. "See, the other day I was walking my Gran's dog. Well, she was her dog." I stumbled over my words, trying to make them come out accurately without giving away too much. I just needed to get this guy to provide an alibi, not give him my life story. So much for that. "Daisy."

"Daisy is your name?"

"I'm Queenie, like I said at the door?" I protested, giving him a look. I didn't feel right at all, getting worse by the minute. "My grandmother. I mean, my dog. *Our* dog is Daisy. My grandmother was killed in our home. That day I waved to you? She . . . died. Just then. While I was out on a walk. I came home and she was dead." The fumes, though faint, were really getting to me. I was thoroughly dizzy despite not having finished even half of my drink. Or maybe it was nerves; the pressure of having to discuss Gran with this stranger. I was saying too much. More than I'd intended. Each word I spoke fell between us like lead. This was not the vibe I'd been going for when I imagined this. An exchange I'd intended to be flirty and constructive was—not.

"That's why I'm here," I said, trying to regroup. I just wanted to get it over with and get home. "There's been some confusion about where I was that day. With the police. Someone in the neighborhood told Detective Barnes—she's in charge of the investigation—that I was at home, and I was wondering if you'd be willing to make a statement saying you saw me go out for a walk?"

"Oh wow, oh no." Damien was shaking his head, an expression of dismay and concern fairly dripping from his symmetrical face. "I'm so sorry, Daisy, to hear all of this. You must be going through such a tough time." He came around the counter, took my elbow, and guided me toward the front door. "I wish I could help you with this. I truly do. And please let me know if I can be of assistance in any other way. But I'm in public relations. There are ethical considerations."

"Excuse me?" I said, baffled. He opened the door at last. Fresh air billowed in, reviving me.

"I can't lie to the police," he said, patting my shoulder like I was a sick llama and he was a dad at a petting zoo who didn't like animals. "And I've never seen you before."

Fourteen

"What a fucking creep!" I exclaimed, banging through the door to find Ben helping Mo cook dinner. The kitchen exuded fresh-picked rosemary from the pot on the windowsill and warming spices like ginger and coriander heating on the stove. The rice cooker steamed on the counter, sending forth the soft, sweet scent of basmati.

I had momentarily forgotten Ben was coming; my mind having blocked out the psychological evaluation and polygraph I had scheduled for the following morning as part of the investigation. For which Ben had offered to help me prepare. The white string lights on the fence around the yard shed a gentle glow over the domestic scene.

Seeing the two of them making food together in my kitchen felt cozy, like family. It helped me squash the odd mixture of shame and confusion I was left with after my interaction with Damien.

I was sure he'd noticed me that day. Why lie about it? When I tried to explain what had happened to my friends, I couldn't. It was as if the words to describe the interaction just dissipated when I tried to grasp them.

And what was up with the jumbled, disconnected state of my mind when I was inside his house? During my walk up the street, my mind cleared fully. But instead of bringing clarity to the situation, my mental sharpness had the opposite effect. It had felt like I was intoxicated, but I'd barely had three sips of that whiskey. If Damien had spiked it with something, which also would not have made sense, the fresh air wouldn't have had me feeling normal within minutes, it would have still been in my system.

What Mo had said earlier—that some people used their talents for the greater good and some didn't—popped into my head. I couldn't explain it, but there was something about Damien that exuded a dark force.

Dinner was a salad, greens, and spiced lentils with rice. As we ate, attempting to talk about semi-normal things like the weather and Ben's cat, I found myself wishing he knew everything about the guardians and about Gran's pendant, and the strange tales her journals spun. However, I doubted that bringing up time travel would reassure anyone about the state of my mental health.

"I have some work to do tonight when we're done prepping for my appointment," I said, taking a bite of collards. "That TV series my ex is working on." Mo and Ben exchanged a look.

"He's paying you?" asked Ben the attorney.

"Not much, but yes. Money! For my writing! I've been waiting for this a long time."

"What was his name again?"

I told him Arlo's full name, surprised when he wrote it down in the little notebook he carried in his pocket.

"Will you have time for your own work?" Mo asked.

"What work? I haven't written a decent word in years," I joked, but it did not feel funny. Mo and Ben seemed to pick up on this. I sighed and tossed my crumpled napkin on the table. "With everything going on . . . I don't know. This is a great opportunity, though. I thought you guys would be excited for me."

"We are," Ben said, glancing at Mo. She nodded, but she didn't meet my eyes. Their feelings about Arlo, or the idea of him, anyway, perhaps weren't much rosier than my own.

"It's just . . ." Mo said, brushing invisible crumbs off the table.

"You have a lot going on," Ben said. "We want the best for you."

"I know," I said. "Thanks. I appreciate you both being here for me so much. Don't know how I'll ever thank you." Then, wanting to change the subject: "Ben, tell me about Gran and your grandmother. How did they meet?"

"Oh," Ben said, putting down his fork. "Anke and Anita, my grandmother, came to the States around the same time, part of a government refugee program. They boarded together at the home of a local Jewish woman who took in refugees from the war. They were hired as Harvey girls together—both learned English very quickly. Anita worked at Union Station too. Until she married my grandpa."

Ben's grandmother was the friend Gran wrote about in her journal. Learning that they had stayed connected for so many years, realizing that connection was living on beyond Gran's death with Ben and I, gave me a sensation I'd never experienced before; like everything is connected. A tragedy of epic proportions brought the two women together, but they were able to transmute that painful experience to form a friendship that was still, even after Gran's death, bearing fruit.

After Ben left, I was eager to get to work on the project for Arlo. It wasn't until I was almost asleep that I remembered I'd forgotten to tell Mo about my interviews with the neighbors and ask her if my thinking might have been muddled from dream-traveling without a license, so to speak.

I tossed and turned all night, so when it got light out I decided to get up early and pick up my paycheck at Vista Mar before my appointment at the police station. I wanted to go to the appointment on my own. Gran had wanted me to be mature and take responsibility for my life. With Mo around, I sensed I ran the risk of relying on her too much, like I had with Gran. After brushing my teeth and throwing on some respectable clothes, I gave Daisy a chewy to keep her busy and snuck out.

My car truly was on its last legs. A rattling emitted from somewhere beneath me and it seemed to get louder each time I drove. With my earnings at the restaurant so far, Wyatt's bribe money, and this week's paycheck, maybe I'd be able to afford a down payment on a used one.

The morning was overcast. Driving through Venice, a thick marine layer coated the windshield. Out along the coast, it cleared up, that hot, thick feeling of sun trying to burn off a fog made the air feel stagnant. The water was steel gray. I shivered just looking at it. The lot at Vista Mar was mostly empty. I recognized Angelo's pickup, and there was a dirty gray delivery truck parked haphazardly near the door to the kitchen. Its doors were flung wide open, the rear gate ajar. I pulled into the lot. It was normal for Angelo to be there early to plan out specials and do the ordering. The truck would be delivering produce or fish, but something about the way it was parked gave me a feeling like something wasn't right.

I parked and got out of the car. I would just get my paycheck and get to my appointment. The ever-changing weather of the morning had turned the ocean blue all the way to the horizon. Now, white surf looked pillowy and soft as it rolled gently in and out. The air was clear and mild, all mist burned away. It was so clear I could see tankers down by El Porto.

I stepped over the curb separating the two parking lots and walked toward the kitchen door. As I got closer, I heard voices through the screen. I made a sharp right turn and ducked behind the dumpsters, hoping I hadn't been seen. A man was telling someone to walk faster, move along. I heard the shuffling footsteps of more than a few people, murmurs in Spanish, then a shriek and a muffled sob. Whoever was inside was in trouble.

The door opened. Angelo, the head chef, walked backward out of it. He held a gun in one hand, with the other he caught the kitchen door and propped it open for the group of people, mostly women and children but a few men, who straggled blinking out into the day as if they'd been somewhere without light. He gestured to the truck with his left hand. I felt a sharp pain at the back of my head. My body lurched sideways. I threw out my arms to catch my fall, but my vision faded before I hit the ground.

Fifteen

I regained consciousness lying on my side on a greasy vinyl floor that smelled of rotten potato skins and fish guts. I remembered enough of hiding behind the dumpster to be scared to move. Without shifting my head, which hurt like hell, I moved my eyes around my field of vision, ascertaining that my body had been moved no farther than the kitchen floor of Vista Mar.

"We can't leave her here," said a chipper female voice, which I recognized as Rita's. "She might go for help."

"Sure we can."

Pirate's baritone was unmistakable.

"We can put her in the office, or the hole. Tie her up."

The hole?

A line of scurrying red ants stretched from the gap between the screen door and the frame, across the vast, disgusting floor, to a crack between the floor and the wall by my head. They were a tiny army, determined to get into that crack. I wondered, my thoughts rising to the surface slowly as if through a haze, what could be so compelling that they'd venture into this nightmare of a place. Ants don't care. They just go after what they want, food. Isn't that what ants like best?

A hand worked its way around my back, another behind my knees. My body was lifted up. I snapped my eyes shut and held my breath. Pirate's seaweed and dust smell filled my nose; I felt the fabric of his T-shirt against the back of my neck. It took all of my concentration to will my muscles slack, my face blank and unconscious.

"She'll wake up soon," Rita said anxiously. "I didn't hit her that hard. Think he'll be mad at me?" *Rita* had knocked me out?

I felt Pirate shake his head. Heard him kick open the screen door. "Long as you didn't do permanent damage," he muttered. "Get the door." Rita's hurried footsteps sounded on sandy asphalt. A car door opened. I was lowered onto a cushioned seat. Something hard, a seatbelt buckle, dug into my shoulder blade. It was all I could do to resist wiggling off it. "See you there," Pirate said. He shut the door. Footsteps crunched on the sandy blacktop around to the driver's side. The car tilted as he got in. I focused on breathing smooth and slow, mimicking sleep.

The car started. Dolly Parton was singing "Light of a Clear Blue Morning;" never was there any more incongruous musical soundtrack to a kidnapping. I was terrified. My mind was all over the place. One minute I was trying to get my hands free and strategizing how to reach the lock so I could throw myself out the door when the car stopped. The next I'd become absorbed in the sounds of the road under the wheels, the sensation of air streaming in an open window, ruffling my hair. A seatbelt buckle dug into my shoulder. The bones of my wrists pressed painfully together behind my back, bound tightly with what felt like scratchy rope. My head ached. My ankle itched. In her quicksilver voice, Dolly assured me that it was all gonna be okay, and I so completely did not believe her. Sweat streamed, soaking the sides of my shirt. The smell coming off me was scared animal.

I hadn't seen Pirate or Rita or any of them since Mo had told me about the guardians. All I knew was that they were on the other side of the rift. Wyatt's side.

I knew Q didn't trust Wyatt. I didn't, however, know if this was because he posed an actual threat, or if it was just dysfunctional family stuff. As far as I knew, they had no idea I'd inherited Gran's abilities. Whatever was going down, I hoped I could use this to my advantage. Lying in Pirate's back seat, I pretended to still be unconscious and prayed that Mo would somehow sense I was in trouble and come find me.

The car pulled in somewhere, coming to a full stop in a patch of shade. By the smells and sounds, I recognized where we were immediately. The rumble and slosh of an idling motor; people talking and shouting in boat language. There wasn't anywhere else like it. The marina, where jankety fishing hacks rubbed shoulders with globe-trotting yachts. Grandad used to have a beautiful little wooden sailboat, the *Regina*, named after me, his only grandchild. He'd take us out on the weekends. Gran sold it after he died.

Pirate killed the engine. "You can sit up, Queenie," he said. Keys dropped in the console, the rustle and crunch of his broad back settling into the leather seat. I stayed quiet, eyes closed. "I know when someone's unconscious and when they're pretending," Pirate said.

He was the guardian of the sea. Of course he knew I was faking it. Various escape plans shuffled through my head. When none of them seemed feasible, I rose, easing my legs to the floor and feeling for the bump on my head, which throbbed. I winced, catching sight of myself in the rearview mirror, where Pirate caught my eye.

"Hi," he said. Was I imagining it, or did he look relieved to see I was somewhat okay? Alive, at least. "Tough break."

"Umm," I managed to get out. So, Pirate wasn't going to assume any responsibility or apologize. My reflection showed slits for eyes and swelling on the right side of my face. I must have hit it when I fell. "'S going on, Pirate? I feel . . . sick." My speech was garbled, and I wasn't pretending. My stomach turned over.

"Hold on," he said, seeing the expression on my face. He opened his door quickly then, hopped out, and came around to the back. Didn't want me to vomit in his nice car, maybe. He reached in and pulled me to my feet. Bending, he put an arm around my waist so I could lean on his shoulder. The salt air made me feel a little better. The nausea receded. But I wasn't going to let Pirate know that. I groaned and doubled over, mock gagging. He held me by both arms, and I pretended to dry heave into the shrubs. But I couldn't pretend to throw up forever. I waited for the next stage of my escape plan to reveal itself to my foggy mind. It didn't.

"I'm okay," I said finally, staggering as I came upright. And it wasn't just acting. I felt awful. I wiped my mouth with the back of my hand. "I'm . . . woozy."

"Time to get on the boat," Pirate said, glancing around. Some people looked our way, but no one made a move to come over. I wondered if I should say I knew about his powers or tell him what Mo had shared with me. But something made me hold back. Playing dumb is often wise when you have no idea what the fuck is going on.

"Boat? I need a hospital," I protested as he led me down the slip to a vintage trawler yacht with forest green trim and a wooden cabin. The motor was running. Wyatt and Rita were seated under an awning on the upper deck. They looked down on me from above, observing my approach like I was some curious species of waterfowl. Though confused and out of sorts, I was sound enough to realize I had placed my head in the lion's mouth, so to speak, by spying on Angelo. Pirate helped me aboard and onto the bottom rungs of steps that more closely resembled a ladder than stairs, then went back down. On the climb to the upper deck, I glimpsed a setup that looked more than livable through the cabin windows. The interior was all polished wood and dark green upholstery, classic and well-kept.

Wyatt nodded in my general direction as I heaved my body from steps to chair over the gently swaying ground. Rita didn't look up from the magazine she was probably pretending to read. I contemplated the risks of jumping overboard.

"A perfect day," Wyatt said, offering me a plastic water bottle from a selection on the bolted-down table. The thought that I might be related to this monster made me even queasier than I already was.

I grunted in response, gingerly taking a seat. No point saying the day was shit. It was just a fact. I reached for the water, then thought better of it and pulled back. In spy movies, hostages with integrity refuse enemy amenities. The water was intended to lull me into a false sense of security, as was Wyatt's comment. I wished so badly in that moment that I had told Mo I was stopping at Vista Mar before my appointment at the police station.

I took the water, unable to resist. It settled my stomach, but not my nerves.

"Why'd you hit me?" I asked Rita, my voice hoarse. But at least I could form a coherent sentence.

Rita stared at me, one eyebrow arched, peach-pink lips pursed. "You watch far too much TV, Queenie," she said. "You hit your head pretty hard when you slipped on the greasy floor. Perhaps we *should* drop you at the hospital when we get back to shore." She tsked like a Stepford mom and returned to her magazine, which featured an emaciated model on the cover and reeked of fragrance. My gut lurched again.

"You fell going into the kitchen," Wyatt said matter-of-factly. The sun, now bright overhead, glinted off the whites of his eyes. "The guys were doing a deep clean this morning. They took up the rubber mats and had just put down degreaser when you walked in."

"That's not true!" I exploded, which made my head split into a new realm of aching. But the hurt didn't stop me. "I hid behind the dumpster because . . ."

"You went in and slipped," Wyatt repeated.

"I didn't! I never made it inside, Wyatt. Then I was all of a sudden waking up on the kitchen floor with ants crawling all over me." I pointed at Rita. "Rita and Pirate were discussing what to do with me. They mentioned 'the hole.' What's the hole, Wyatt? And who were those people being herded into a delivery truck? And why was Angelo shouting at them? And why did he have a gun?" I sat back, arms crossed tightly over my chest.

Ants. I'd seen ants crawling under the wall. Ants crawled places for food. The wall. The people. The hole. Shen. What had Shen said about people going missing? Pieces were coming together too slowly in my mind. I was right on the edge of making sense of it, but my thinking wasn't linear or clear. In retrospect, I realize I was probably suffering from a severe concussion.

"I understand you were supposed to go for a psychiatric evaluation today," Wyatt said. "What's it for?"

I sucked in a breath. How could he . . . ?

"You put me down as your employer on the forms," he continued. "You gave them permission to contact your employer, for collateral information."

I had done no such thing. Had I?

"I need to get off. This fucking boat," I said through gritted teeth. I looked down. Pirate was tying off the line he had released from the dock. My heart started beating fast, skipped a beat, then another. The boat was about to *leave*.

"No need to use such strong language, Queenie. We're trying to help you," Wyatt said, completely ignoring my questions about Angelo and the gun and the people. "I'm afraid you're in no condition to go off on your own right now," Wyatt said. "We took you aboard so we could watch you, make sure you're okay."

"You could have taken me to the hospital."

"Do you want to go to the hospital? Queenie, *what exactly* do you imagine would be the outcome of a psych eval?" He was staring at me like he knew something about me I didn't, like he was trying to intimidate me. All I wanted was off the boat. And for my head to stop spinning. And to feel safe. I didn't answer. I didn't want to go to the hospital. Nor did I want to keep my appointment at the police station. What I wanted was to curl up in bed with an ice pack and pretend none of this was happening. I wanted Gran to sit by me and tell me everything was going to be okay. Indeed, what *would* happen if a psychologist gained access to my inner thoughts? I was paranoid my new boss was a murderer, was convinced the moon was living in my house, and had recently become acquainted with time-traveling, existence-weaving, earthquake-controlling deities who fixed cars and made the best elote I'd ever tasted.

"Pirate's a trained emergency responder." Rita's voice broke through my thoughts. She lazily turned a page of her magazine. "Coast Guard. You'll be fine."

I'll be fine, I thought, looking around. Yeah, right. There were deep-sea fishing poles in holders on the lower aft deck. Heavy steel hooks glinted against lead sinkers. The flexible poles bounced as the boat began to move, vibrating with the motor. A line of old brightly painted clapboard shops and restaurants taunted me from shore with their decrepit yet cheery facades. We were moving steadily further from the relative safety of land.

Still not too far to swim.

A power boat sped by, packed with screaming drunk people blasting club music. A charter fishing boat pursued by sea lions crawled past on its way in, a few of the guys leaning over the edge to check out the bikini-clad dancers. We slid past the jetty and entered the bay; the beach was far enough away that the people on the shore looked mini. A pelican with a six-foot wingspan dive bombed the rolling surface of the water, emerging with its catch visibly wriggling around inside the pouch of its beak. As the bird pitched its head back to swallow, I commiserated with the doomed fish.

"Where are we going?" I asked Wyatt.

"I have to take some photos. It's a work thing."

"Oh?" I said. I wondered what percentage of Wyatt's work activities were legitimate. I wondered if the boat played a role in what I'd witnessed earlier. Mexico wasn't so far away by water. "You all go out often?"

"It's Pirate's boat," Rita said. "He takes us out sometimes. He lives on it." Of course he did.

The air was moist and warm. Wind blew in swirls that made me feel like I was inside of something soft, like sponge cake or cotton candy. I breathed deeply, attempting to make my mind calm. I wouldn't be able to do anything if I couldn't gain control over my thoughts.

Wyatt lit a cigarette.

Beachgoers were now the size of small insects. From the bay, I could clearly see the film of smog hovering over the city, covered over by an umbrella of clear blue above the filthy line. I tried not to breathe in Wyatt's secondhand smoke until I realized there was no smell. An onshore breeze was steadily picking up, transforming the stillness, presumably blowing away the smoke. But . . . something strange was happening to the smog. The rhythm of Wyatt breathing and the boat's smooth passage through the water and the mild but constant throbbing in my skull had me mesmerized. I could have sworn that as he breathed in, the layer of smog seemed to flow toward us. As he breathed out, streaky clean white clouds multiplied on the horizon. I sat there quietly, swept up in a trance-like state, enchanted by the rhythm and flow of air and smoke and sea.

I don't know how much time passed before Pirate's boots sounded on the ladder.

"Nearly there," he said, joining us. Where? I wondered. But didn't dare ask. I was confused by the sound of someone else coming up the ladder. But weren't we all here on the upper deck? When Angelo emerged over the top rung I almost fell off my chair.

"What the—!"

"Hush, Queenie," Rita said without even looking up from her magazine. "You'll hurt yourself. Best to stay calm."

Angelo greeted me like nothing was amiss and handed Wyatt a fancy-looking camera with a zoom lens.

"Here you go," he said. "Should be all set."

"Should be– or is all set?" Wyatt asked irritably.

"All set," Angelo shot back.

Wyatt nodded and tossed his smoldering cigarette stub overboard. Pirate retreated to the wheel and Rita, Angelo, and Wyatt followed him down to the bow. I moved to stand at the rail to watch them. We were coming up on a hulking structure jutting out of the ocean's surface, an oil rig—or I wasn't sure what else it could be. I'd never seen one up close. It was a singular point of ugliness in the expanse of green-gray water and sunshine. Metal gauges and pipes protruded from the beastly contraption. The metal was dingy, dead seeming, at extreme odds with its surroundings. As we got closer, I could make out a black and red logo printed on one smooth section of steel. I remembered back to the men I'd served at Vista, the oil company executives. This must be one of theirs. Wyatt was snapping photos of the different components and Rita was taking notes on a clipboard. Angelo looked on, his posture defensive. He definitely wasn't at ease. Wyatt appeared to finish taking photos and handed the camera to Rita, who hung it around her neck. I leaned my elbow on the rail and stretched my back. Once they were done, we'd head back to land, and I would quit my job. If I had to give Wyatt back his bribes to get him to leave me alone, I would. I'd even promise not to go to the authorities. I just wanted to go home and forget I ever heard of Vista Mar. Wyatt and Angelo were standing in the bow, facing each other. Wyatt appeared to be explaining something to Angelo, who was looking increasingly alarmed. The wind in my ears and waves slapping the sides of the trawler prevented me from hearing what they were saying. But I didn't care. I was done with this. I would tell Mo about it, and if she and Q and the others felt like doing something about it, they could. Like Shen, I was out. I'd even give my pendant to Mo. I would go back to school. I'd study to be a teacher or a real estate agent or something. It didn't matter. I just wanted to feel normal again.

"Did you ever really feel normal, though?" Pirate said from behind me. I startled and turned, pressing my back against the rail. The volume and intensity of Wyatt and Angelo's exchange had increased so that I could catch snippets of their argument. The words "cartel" and "smuggling" and a lot of cursing drifted on the wind.

"Excuse me?" Had I been talking to myself?

"No, you weren't talking to yourself," Pirate said. He moved toward me, and I was struck with a fear that he would push me over the rail, which I gripped tightly with both hands. I crouched, ready to fight, for all the good it would have done. Pirate put his hands up palms facing me. "It's okay, Queenie. I'm not going to hurt you."

"You read my mind." A violation of my privacy. Or was it? I felt so alone, maybe I—

"Only because you let me." His smile was warm and reached his eyes. A crack split the air behind me. When I turned, Rita was lowering a pistol. Wyatt was standing on the lower rung of the bow rail staring over at the spreading red cloud in the water, which was all that could be seen of what was left of Angelo. I think I screamed. Pirate was holding me tightly around my shoulders. If he hadn't been, I would have fallen to the deck. Was I next?

"I came up because I thought that might happen," Pirate said, shaking his head sadly. He was so close I could feel his breath on my ear. "I didn't want you to freak out." He helped me to sit with my back against the rail. As if to hold myself together, I wrapped my arms around my bent knees. Pirate knelt beside me, continuing to speak in a low, soothing voice. "Angelo was a bad guy. Rita had no choice. Wyatt confronted him about something. You know that deal Shen's been going on about? Angelo pulled a gun on him. He was working for a cartel, Queenie. We didn't know for sure until today, but—"

"Who were those people? The ones who came out of the kitchen?" I was shaking like a leaf and my voice shook, too.

"We help people from Mexico and Latin America who need to escape to safety. We run a group up from Mexico on my boat every few months. Angelo was helping us with that operation. But he turned dirty. A few months ago, Shen got a weird phone call and became suspicious. Apparently, a cartel had recruited him. We were paying him to take people from a safe room at Vista Mar, north—to Canada, mostly. They go through known, trusted channels to establish new identities and try to start over. The cartel was paying him to redirect them."

"Oh my god," I said. "Like, human trafficking?"

Pirate nodded. "We lost one group . . . That's what Shen was so upset about."

"Wh-why should I believe you?" I asked, still shaking. "Rita just killed a man... just shot him. Like it was nothing."

Pirate sat back on one heel. "We fund these trips," he sighed. "It's not cheap. Shen was concerned about the financial losses Angelo's activities posed, and even more worried about the people who seemed to go missing somewhere between Los Angeles and the Canadian border."

"Oh," I said in a small voice. "Shen's like a whistleblower."

"Yeah, like that," Pirate confirmed.

I was sure Q didn't know about any of this. He thought Wyatt was selfish and corrupt. If what Pirate was saying was true, Q had his kid pegged all wrong. If Wyatt was his kid, and I could trust any of them were who they said they were, which was increasingly doubtful.

"I know you know more about us than you're letting on," Pirate continued. "You only have the story from one side. It isn't the whole story."

"I would be happy," I said through chattering teeth, "if I never saw any of you again."

"Suit yourself," Pirate said, standing. "Let me know if you change your mind and want to talk."

It was too much. Angelo's sudden, violent death brought the moments in the kitchen with Gran's body flooding back. I hadn't liked Angelo. In my gut, I knew Pirate was telling me the truth. It didn't matter, though. I couldn't make peace with what had just occurred. Tears dripped off my chin, wetting my shirt, but I couldn't feel or hear myself crying. I felt like a formless blob of blood, guts, and grief puddled on the deck of that boat. I couldn't fathom how I'd ended up there, that this was my life. I had never felt so alone. I reached up to touch the black stone that hung around my neck. It responded with its customary vision-blurring effect. I had to know what had happened to Gran. It was the only thing that could fix this. I pressed the pads of my fingertips into the stone, which was warm from being against my skin.

Time traveling poses far greater risks, consequences you couldn't even begin to comprehend, Mo had said. Well, that was a chance I was willing to take. Trouble was, I didn't know how to do it. Dream-travel happened passively, by touching an object that evoked a dream. Time travel, I suspected, would be more active. I closed my eyes and closed both palms across the pendant. I focused every bit of strength I had left on that day when I'd left Gran at the house and taken Daisy for a walk.

I slipped out of present time and into a dreamscape. Then, I pushed further. Time traveling feels like walking to the edge of a cliff without looking right or left, only in the direction of your intent, which you can't see, but you know where it is, and leaping off.

I'm there, that day, across the street from my house, watching myself leave through the kitchen door with Daisy. The lace curtains next door shiver, then fall back into place.

I note my outfit; jeans, navy blue running shoes, forest green hooded sweatshirt. I watch myself wave to the man in the suit, Damien. I watch as I disappear down the road.

The sun settles steadily in the sky to the west until it hovers just above the line of the horizon. The mountains in the distance are a smoky purple, in harmony with the woodsmoke rising from the bungalow's chimney. Gran has lit a fire. If I could only go to her, see her one last time. But I must not. It could ruin everything. As painful as it is, I need to wait. Besides, I'm not really me. I am future me, which is different from present day me.

I am confused.

The street is quiet. A car passes, pulls into a driveway up the street. The lace curtain pulls all the way back and I see the pale orb of cactus garden lady's curious face. She stares hard in my direction, blinks, then shakes her head and looks away, as if I was there and then not. Perhaps this was why she told the detective she'd seen me. She must have been confused, seeing me leave, then thinking maybe she saw me crouching in the shadows across the street. I admit, it's strange behavior. But how well can she see me? I pass a hand in front of my face. Through it, I can still see the bungalow. I am both here and not here. Real and not real.

I step further back into the shadow cast by the tree, doing my best to will myself fully invisible. Anyway, now I know Damien saw me, which makes him either a liar or a person with a terrible memory.

Then I see something that makes me gasp. My heart races and butterflies take over my gut and I am dizzy again, a sensation that is becoming all too familiar.

I am walking up the street. Real me. Solid me. Except something is off. I'm wearing a hooded sweatshirt but it's black, not green. The shoes are charcoal gray.

Not possible. I went for a long walk, yet there I am, much too soon after I left—no Daisy in sight. Where is Daisy? She never would have let me come home by myself. But there is no mistaking that it is me who is walking up to the front door. Am I high? Or was I? I racked my memory. I'd been stressed before the walk. What if I'd found something lying around in my room, a leftover pill? A pill that made me forget what happened after I took it. No.

I never use the front door, yet somehow, I am there trying the door handle and then there is Gran opening the door, which must have been locked, and she is looking at me in confusion and I hear her asking: "Where is Daisy?"

That is not me. It looks a lot like me, but it isn't me.

Gran tries to shut the door. She knows something is wrong, that it is not me. It is not me. I want to go to her, to run over and beat this impostor into the ground but I am frozen. Against Gran's protests, I watch body-snatcher-me push the door open. I hear the shattering of crystal on brick before the door slams shut and still, my body will not obey my command to get up. Because I am inside the house with Gran. It was me all along. Or was it?

The front door opens. I walk out. Or, rather, Gran pushes someone who looks a heck of a lot like me out onto the front walk.

"Don't come back, Rita," she shouts. "I should never have sent Queenie to Vista Mar. She quits. Do you hear me? Make sure you tell Wyatt what I said!"

Rita. Wyatt.

I did not hurt Gran. As far as I could tell, *Rita* did not hurt Gran. The attack must have happened after Gran expelled Rita-as-Queenie from the bungalow.

But they were involved, they had something to do with it.

I try to stay in it, I really do. I want to run across the street. I want to stop whatever is about to happen. But Time grabs and pulls me. It feels like a riptide, impossible to resist. Right before Time engulfs me, I see someone walking up the street. Whoever it is, a dark shape, I can't make it out in the waning light.

That is the murderer. Instinctively, I know this to be true.

Everything in me screams warning. *Swim sideways, Queenie!* It's Grandad's voice. There he is, splashing fully dressed into the water, his hands cupped around his mouth, eyes trained on me. A lifeguard is running down the beach, diving toward me with one of those red floaty things. I lose sight of Grandad and the lifeguard as water fills my eyes and nose and mouth. I blow a fierce breath out, kick up and over as hard as I can, trying to find which way is out. The current releases me with a sucking sound, like it doesn't want to let go.

I opened my eyes, pried my clenched fingers from around Gran's pendant. Through a small round portal above my head, I saw the night sky, black as the stone around my neck, studded with stars. Someone has me wrapped in blankets and put a damp cloth over my forehead.

Without moving, I tried to recall exactly what I'd seen. I couldn't parse it out. Nothing made sense. I left and then I was back, without Daisy. But it wasn't me. It was Rita, in disguise. It looked like me. But whoever looked like me had not killed Gran. She'd thrown me/Rita out. But it explained what the witnesses saw. Seeing Gran alive broke something loose in me, a flood of grief so deep I thought I might pass out again.

". . . some kind of seizure," a voice was saying. "Maybe she's epileptic. But if I didn't know any better, I'd say she's one of us. Wait—could she be? Anke was . . ." So, Pirate hadn't shared his knowledge of my powers with Rita and Wyatt. There was a rustle of cloth, the creaking of leather as someone shifted in their chair. A woman, Rita again. Always seeming to be there when I was emerging from a stupor. I rolled over so I could see the room. The three of them sat in tan leather chairs in the main cabin in the dim light that flickered as the boat rocked gently. In response to my movement, they turned in unison in my direction.

I didn't want to be there. I no longer thought Wyatt might have killed Gran, no longer thought he was simply a villain. Despair had me in its grasp. I realized, with numb shock, that I no longer cared if I lived or died.

"Please," I called as weakly as I could. It wasn't an act. "I need air."

Pirate came and, without speaking, lifted me, still wrapped in the blanket, and carried me out of the cabin. It was night. The stars, so indistinct when on land in the city, stood out against a tar-black expanse of sky that faded into a blueish-black halo around a perfectly full moon.

"Whatever you saw, don't be so sure it's what you think it is," Pirate said quietly, under his breath, so the others wouldn't hear. I put a wall up around my thoughts.

"Hmm," I said. He lowered me gently onto a cushioned bench. "Do you have any hot tea?" Pirate hesitated, then nodded.

"You stay right there," he said. "Don't move."

"Where would I go?"

As soon as he had disappeared into the galley kitchen, I wadded the blanket on the bench to make it look like I was huddled underneath it and slid as quietly as I could over the stern rail. The water was exactly as cold and dark as I deserved it to be, but I didn't cry out as its icy fingers slid over my warm belly. The rest was easy. All I had to do was reach shore. I didn't know how long I'd been unconscious, but we couldn't be far. Once I got there, I didn't know what I would do. The thought of going back to the bungalow felt wrong. I needed to figure out what had happened with the me I saw entering the front door right before Gran died. I felt all mixed up about what was magic and what was normal, and how that all fit into what I had previously understood to be a constant, which was reality. Part of me wanted to never go home again. What if I didn't? Just disappeared like my mother. If I did, I'd never have to sort through it all. I could get rid of Gran's pendant and pretend I was normal, that I had no responsibilities . . . Couldn't I? Part of me suspected that would not be as easy or possible as I'd like to think. If there was something I'd learned over the past few weeks, it was that the past might take a while to catch up with you, but it always does. All the new information was overwhelming, and not knowing who to trust was exhausting. I just wanted to be alone.

I did not care if I made it to shore alive, was aware I probably wouldn't.

I swam toward the moon. The cool glow infused the dark water with a mercurial silver light. I swam until I began to feel more warm than cold and then I swam further. How much time passed before I heard shouts from the boat, looking for me. I didn't look back. I stroked and kicked, breathing so deeply and rhythmically that I couldn't cry or stop or think until I began to imagine music, a high singing from below. My muscles began to fatigue. I could feel them acutely, each one, surrendering to exhaustion. I floated, images from my life drifting across the vast dark. Roller-skating along the bike path by the ocean. Crying when a Dodgers cap that I didn't take off for all of sixth grade flew off in the wind out on Grandad's sailboat. Watching little kids get on and off the carousel while I ate a hot dog on a stick. Throwing myself into the crashing waves at the beach when I was happy, sad, lonely, confused, angry. Watching the weather from the bluffs. My life was wrapped around the sea, or was it wrapped around me?

A soft thing brushed against my leg. I cried out, imagining shark fins cutting circles around me. A smooth roundish thing rose from the water beside me and bumped my shoulder, chattered, prodded me again.

Dolphins.

They flowed through water like living reams of gray silk. They pressed against my belly, transferring the warmth of their bodies to mine. I had no strength to fight against their goodwill; all I could do was surrender. When the last muscle gave way and my mind went numb from cold and I began to sink like a stone, they floated me from below, one bearing the weight of my body, then passing me off to another, and in this way, they ferried me across the tides, which seemed to swell as the moon appeared larger and larger until it was joined with the earth and the water in a great swirling mass. *Whatever you saw, don't be so sure it's what you think it is.* Pirate's warning circled in my mind even as I surrendered.

Surfers found me somewhere between dreaming and waking on the dry sand of the beach in the morning just before sunrise. A man and a woman, afraid at first that I was dead, roused me from my half-conscious state and helped me stand. The woman handed me a phone. My first instinct was to dial the bungalow. Mo would answer. She would walk down to the beach to get me. I could go home.

Except I couldn't.

I couldn't face . . . anyone. This left me with few options.

"I'll walk, thanks. It's not far."

I handed the phone back, observing my own trembling hand as if from a distance as I passed it to her. She saw it too and, probably thinking I was chilled, passed me a bright blue towel.

"Keep it," she said. "I've got another one."

Strangely, I wasn't even very cold. I should have drowned. But I was very much alive. I was not, however, well. I couldn't face going home or to Vista Mar. So, I chose neither.

Sixteen

It's amazing, in a city built for cars, how far you can get on foot.

All it takes is time.

As I trudged along trash-strewn roadways, through underpasses holding my breath against urine and excrement vapors from homeless encampments, past well-kept houses on leafy tree-lined streets, I did my best not to think. If I'd had any money, I probably would have ducked into one of the seedy liquor stores I passed and bought a bottle of something, because that's what people do. It's what I'd have done if I had money. Several times, passing the encampments, I imagined the goodies its residents might have stashed in their pockets or hidden in the busted vans and tents bursting with worldly possessions. I had made a promise to Gran to stay clean. You'll suffer more alive, a cruel voice in the back of my mind suggested. Countered by: *Life is precious and so are you.* That was a memory of Gran's voice. Words she'd said to me many times when I despaired and didn't see any reason to keep trying. Depression had plagued me since I was a child. I knew it well. It was why I'd spent so much time trying to escape from my own mind, my dull reality. I could feel my reptile brain craving instant gratification, a quick release from pain, bargaining with my grief, my heart, the part of me that knew I could still make Gran proud even though she was dead. Despite my mistakes.

My clothes, hair, and skin dried stiff with salt. The day was hot. I paused on an overpass to look down at the Los Angeles River through a chain-link fence that left rusty smudges on my fingers, its meager trickle trapped in concrete. A snowy egret cooled her feet in the water, dignified as a crane in a Japanese watercolor landscape. What drew her to this place? The traffic, smog, and waste seemed not to faze her. The air shimmered. A heat mirage? I blinked. Still there. Sweat beading on my temples and upper lip evaporated almost immediately. When I felt my skin beginning to burn, I draped the azure towel over my head.

Dehydrated, footsore, ears ringing from traffic and city noise, I reached Central Library in the late afternoon. The vast foyer was cool and quiet. The tree flesh and ink smell of books that hits high in the back of the nose and settles behind the eyes. Footsteps and hushed voices echoed off the stone floor. I went straight to the restrooms, remembering there was a drinking fountain nearby. City water had never tasted so good. I let it run over my cracked lips. In the bathroom, I wiped my skin down with damp paper towels, used the toilet. Pulling my stiff denim shorts back on was an unwelcome challenge. For a moment, I wished I was home, then pushed the thought away. Here, in a public bathroom that served as a personal bathhouse to many of downtown's homeless population, I could avoid looking in the mirror hanging above the sink.

 I could barely look at my reflection, never mind go home. Mo and the others would be angry with me for time traveling. I was sure they already knew. She'd mentioned something about ripples in creation, which was how Q tracked things in his vague, ambiguous way. I wondered if what I'd done had messed anything up irrevocably. I couldn't go to work and face Rita and Wyatt, even Pirate, whom I trusted the most of all of them. Who knew what they'd be capable of doing to me to keep me quiet? I just couldn't condone what they had done, no matter how bad Angelo was. The time travel had also affected me mentally. I kept having flashbacks of finding Gran's body—the blue tile in the kitchen, the corner of the counter where the report said Gran hit her head as she fell backward. When it happened, my legs had buckled beneath me. Now, cool gray tiles met my cheek. Water. I'd be okay once I hydrated, I thought, dragging my body up from the floor by bracing my hands on the steel edge of a wastebasket mounted into the wall. Some food, maybe, would help. I had no money, no phone. Shakily, holding myself against the sink, I bent to retrieve my towel from the floor where I'd collapsed. As I rose again, I allowed my eyes to flick to the mirror. Dreams and nightmares stitched together in a mask pretending to look like me. I splashed water over my face and hair one more time. How does one survive on the streets?

 I found a shaded place under a palm tree looking out on Flower Street and a discarded paper cup. People are often kind. What struck me the most was their lack of curiosity. I was just another homeless person to them. Me and so many others. I looked around at the various other wanderers, all of them, as far as I could tell, far deeper into the lifestyle than myself. Some seemed to carry their homes on their backs. Some looked like they carried the weight of the world on their shoulders. Others looked like they were on vacation, burnt dark from the sun and lounging; or hustling for change, or just resting in the shade. Over there was madness, screaming, shaking its fist at a lamppost. The vet who can't erase what happened or make sense of it. The wizened face with a mind stuck in some youthful nightmare.

By the time the sun began to set, I had accumulated enough coins for a hot dog from a cart down the block. Despite my gnawing hunger, it was sawdust in my mouth. Eventually, I fell asleep, huddled against the rustling palm, which I'd begun to think of as mine. It was my piece of the earth that no longer held anything for me. Much later, I jerked awake as the icy beam of a flashlight swept over my body, lingering on my face, checking for signs of life—or death, I suppose. Cops, I determined. It moved away when my eyes clenched against the light. In the street-glow velvet of very late night, I wrapped the salty towel more tightly around my shoulders to hide my features. I would be reported missing at some point. Maybe I had been already. There was more than one reason the LAPD might want to find me.

How long later? Still night. The towel is ripped from around my shoulders. Something cold and hard is pressed to my throat, daring me not to scream. Rank stench of weeks-old body odor and hot, sour breath. I gasp and a moist hand clamps on my mouth, a hand which I bite until blood pours over my bottom lip. A howl of pain pierces my eardrum, my throat is released, and I run. Adrenaline courses through my limbs. I am halfway up the library steps when I realize no one is following me. Breathing hard, I collapse to the ground. I grasp my pendant out of habit, for comfort.

My vision shimmers. The scene breaks.

It is sunset, the sky is pink over Flower Street, the sun going down to the west in an impressionist painting of orange, purple, red. Cars going by are vintage. People dressed in old-fashioned clothes. I'm seated cross-legged on a woven purple blanket spread on a square of pavement near the base of the steps leading up to the faux Egyptian building. The library is just the same. I look down at my hands. My hands. Anke's hands. We are holding the cards. The ones Gran willed to Althea (even though she is gone). I flip over the top card, fully expecting to see The Devil leering at me. Instead, it's the Queen of Swords in a tower room with windows overlooking snow-capped mountains and a lake, sword in hand.

When I came to, I slowly sat up, checking my body all over. Clothes intact. Towel gone. I rise and limp to the palm tree where I was assaulted in the night, taking a moment to mourn the loss of my blue towel. It was the only item of comfort I had. I sustained some bruises in the scuffle, but ... I'm fine. I leaned back, resting my head on the rough hide of my angel tree who forgot to keep watch, pulled my knees up against my chest, and wrapped them with my arms. The air was cool. My skin was clammy and carried a hint of the noxious smell of the man I'd fought off. I pulled up handfuls of grass from the ground and rubbed my arms and legs and chest with it to erase the unwelcome odor.

The library opened at ten. A man with graying hair was stacking books at the circulation desk. I straightened my filthy pink sweater, tucked my hair behind my ears. Asked him if I could use the phone. "Local call?" he asked, handing me a portable handset without even looking at me. I nodded. "Keep it short." He scanned the barcode on a book, studied the spine, put it down so I could see the title. *King Lear.* He looked at me and smiled, pushed the book toward me. "Have you read it? The scene where they're out in the storm on the heath . . . spectacular."

"I've read it," I said, trying not to move my face too much. My voice is a dry croak. "Betrayal, madness, no clear resolution."

He raised his eyebrows. "Much like life."

The librarian transferred *King Lear* to a stack. "Take your time with the phone." I considered calling Mo, or Ben. They would understand. They cared about me. They would help me. But could I face them, knowing what I now knew? I dialed.

Arlo picked up on the fourth ring. "Come get me?" I pleaded.

"Who is this?" He was the only person I felt fit to see.

"Me. Queenie."

"Is it morning?"—his groggy reply.

"*Please,* Arlo."

I had been hiding out in Arlo's apartment for two days. Three? Four? Thanks to a diet consisting mainly of spaghetti with sauce from a jar and gin and tonics, I'd lost track.

After Arlo came to pick me up at the library, he brought me back to his apartment. I paced his kitchen for what seemed like hours. Then I sat on the dirty bathroom floor, crying. To his credit or his detriment, Arlo didn't ask questions. Nor did he comply when I asked him for just a little something. "I don't do all that anymore, Reginald," he said, shaking his head. "Remember how I almost killed you?" I hadn't realized the incident had made such an impact on him. And there I was thinking he only thought about himself. "Annnd, it's a condition of my probation," he clarified. Aha.

After I stopped crying, he handed me a small stack of twenties for the pages I'd emailed him: two hundred dollars. Not much, but more than I'd ever earned by my "pen" before. Once my nerves settled down some, I was able to sit on the couch with an old laptop he lent me. I told him I wanted to keep working on the pilot project.

Obviously, I could never return to work at Vista Mar.

Surprisingly, what came out when I started typing was not on the topic of a high-school football player who sustains a severe concussion and switches bodies with a nerd. Instead, I was writing about a young Roma woman who survives years in a Nazi concentration camp, leaves Europe for Los Angeles to begin a new life, and quickly finds herself embroiled in the terrifying, beautiful chaos of her new city in ways she never could have imagined. It was a love story and a thriller, with an undercurrent of the fantastic. My teeth sank into the meat of it—not that I wanted to think about teeth sinking into the meat of anything. When Arlo was home all I could do was lie on the couch that doubled as my bed and stare at the muted TV. But when he was out, I wrote feverishly, not stopping to eat or drink or even pee.

One morning I was caught up in one of my trance-like writing sessions when there was a knock at the door. I rose from the sofa, back and bladder protesting, and went to look through the peephole. Ben stood a respectful distance from the door, looking disheveled, like he hadn't slept for days. His black hair was extra shaggy. Behind his glasses, which glinted in the yellow light from the hall window, his easygoing gray eyes appeared puffy and red, his shoulders tense and hunched.

I was struck by the realization that he was probably here looking for me. Warmth flooded my chest.

Until I thought about going home, facing *everything*. I tiptoed back to my nest, willing him to go away. Shh. Nobody home. If I didn't answer the door, Ben would eventually leave, and I would be left alone with Arlo and his collection of 90s-era action figures and the knowledge that one day soon, whether in hours or days or weeks, the police would find me. I would be tried for murder, and I would probably be found either guilty or declared insane. *But Detective Barnes, Rita, this chick I work with, is a shapeshifter. She* stole *my identity.*

Until then, I would write.

Then I heard loud footsteps on the stairs. Ben stopped knocking and calling my name. Arlo's voice out on the landing talking to Ben: "Hey, man, can I help you?"

"I'm looking for Queenie. She here?"

"Who are you?"

"Her lawyer." That wasn't strictly true. He was Gran's lawyer. "Her friend, too."

A pause. I'd told Arlo no one could know where I was, that people might be looking for me. He'd agreed to give me some time, then added: *But you'll have to figure your shit out, whatever it is, soon. I mean . . . unless you want to get back together?*

Noooo.

I'd been evasive in response. By evasive I mean that I'd fallen face down on the couch, pulled a musty cushion over my head, and stayed there until he left the room. I guess he was growing tired of me cluttering up his living room and cramping his sex life though, because he barely took a beat before giving me up to Ben.

"Yeah. She's here." Oh no. And worse, he had questions. "You know why she's here? At first, I thought maybe she wanted to get back with me, but . . ." I could almost see Arlo's halfhearted shrug through the closed door. I couldn't for the life of me figure out why he would want to be with me when he obviously cared so little. I shook my head. "She's got that house to herself now, right?" Arlo asked.

"She actually has someone living with her," Ben replied, his voice calm. "Things got . . . complicated after her grandmother passed away. She's had to deal with a lot." The sound of Arlo sorting through his keys. I held my breath. Nowhere to go, no place to hide. "She had an important appointment a few days ago that she didn't show up for . . . Mo—that's her housemate—and I think it all just got to be too much."

"And what's she to you?"

An edge of jealousy had crept into Arlo's tone.

"Like I said, I'm her lawyer."

"Why would Queenie need a lawyer to go around looking for her?"

Hello, I'm right here. I can hear you.

I waited for Ben to betray me too, for him to tell Arlo I was a suspect in Gran's murder investigation. That I was required by law to present myself for questioning when I was summoned.

"Lots of people are worried about her, me included. I—I need to know she's okay . . . Is she?"

When Arlo opened the door, tears were streaming down my cheeks. I wiped them away, but they kept coming. Ben came straight across the room, crouched down, and wrapped his arms around me. Unable to resist, I leaned into him, breathing in the musk of his skin, laundry detergent, and the aged teak and Darjeeling aroma of his office.

"Let me take you home," he said.

"I can't."

He pulled back, holding me at arm's length. Arlo was leaning on the doorframe, watching us.

"You want to stay here?"

I shook my head no, then yes, then no again.

Arlo rolled his eyes. "Just go with him, Queenie," he said, his exasperation apparent. "I have a deadline and this," he made a circle motion with his hand at me and Ben, "this drama is not helping. You just called me up the other day because you're running away from something more interesting, like you do. You *always* sell yourself short and get in your own way."

Ben and I both looked at him in surprise.

"Just go. You can take the laptop."

"Arlo," I started to protest, but he held up a hand to stop me.

"Yeah, yeah, I know you're not doing work for me," he said dismissively. "I looked at it last night while you were sleeping. It's okay. It's really *good* stuff, actually."

"You're not paying her for the work she did for you, anyway," Ben said. Arlo's eyebrows shot up.

"What do you mean?" I asked Ben. "He paid me the other day."

"Remember we talked about him when he offered you the work? I thought I remembered coming across his name somewhere. *He*," Ben pointed at Arlo, "landed a contract with UniPix last month."

"You said . . ."

Arlo swept the scrum of random keys and paper and pens off the straight-backed chair next to the door that doubled as an entry table. He sat.

"I choked," he said, staring at the floor. "I wrote the pilot, landed the contract. Then I choked when it was time to deliver the script for the second episode."

"The one I finished last week?" I asked, jumping to my feet. "The one you paid me *two hundred* dollars for?" Arlo stared at the floor, unable to meet my eyes. "You *said* you would credit me if it went through! You said it was still under consideration and I was writing it just in case. You *promised* me decent pay if you got a contract!"

"I—was planning to. For future work, anyway," he said. "See, I psyched myself out and needed a boost to get through a bad patch of writer's block

. . ." His voice trailed off as his gaze swept the room, coming to rest on a vintage G.I. Joe on the windowsill that had featured in my nightmares over the past few days. It seemed to give him the courage to continue with his confession. "I couldn't credit you for this episode because then they would think *I* couldn't personally deliver . . . creatively, you know? I sank all of my savings into the pilot. Most of the advance went to that. I swear I was going to tell you and make it up to you," he finished lamely.

"You should have told me. I would have understood."

"Really?" he asked.

I shrugged. No, probably not. I nodded anyway.

Arlo straightened, stretching his long legs out in front of him, finally meeting my eyes. "I was embarrassed. And I wasn't sure I could get it together. Didn't want you to get your hopes up if it was all just going to come crashing down."

I'd spent the entirety of my relationship with Arlo feeling envious of him while simultaneously cutting him down to size in my head, resenting the successful image he always played up. I'd felt like he was using me, but as was becoming clear, I was no better than him on that front. He liked how my looks and my bright ideas reflected on him and I liked how his successes reflected on me. But we didn't really enjoy each other's company. And he *was* legitimately successful, by some standards, anyway. He was an artist working on a project that meant something to him and it had sprouted wings. Even as his career seemed like it was about to take off, he had managed to steer himself down a self-defeating rabbit hole. Guess we weren't so different after all.

I sighed and looked at Ben.

Maybe Arlo was right, that I had a habit of getting in my own way. He, apparently, did too. But I wasn't going to point it out to him. I was done competing with him in that way. I was also done being his writing minion.

"Thanks for putting me up, Arlo," I said. "Really, I mean it." I stood and began to gather the few belongings not already on my person, which consisted exactly of a sweater ingrained permanently with sand and the laptop that contained the beginnings of my manuscript. "And for this." I forced a smile as I tucked the computer under my arm. "I'll consider it payment for services rendered. You're both right. Time for me to go home."

"No hard feelings?" Arlo asked, half standing. I motioned for him to sit. I wasn't in the mood for awkward hugs.

"Nope," I said.

"I could use some help with the next episode," he said. "I'll . . . do all the things I said I would before."

"Nope," I said, "I'm good."

I wasn't, but it was a start.

Seventeen

"Where's Mo?" I asked once I was buckled into the passenger seat of Ben's car with Daisy in my lap. She covered my face with kisses, then leaned her head on my shoulder.

"Daisy missed you," Ben grinned. "Can you tell?"

"Not as much as I missed her," I cooed, ruffling her soft ears. She buried her head into my armpit, making me want to cry again.

He turned the key in the ignition, looked behind for oncoming traffic. "I came here to look for you, thinking you might have . . ." He trailed off. Ben was hard to read but he didn't think very highly of Arlo, I could tell that much. "Mo took the bus to Vista Mar to see if you were there. We were worried about you."

"Oh no!" I said, sitting forward. "We have to go after her."

"Whoa, okay," Ben said, turning into a gap in traffic. He glanced at me, obviously wondering why his mention of the restaurant had made me panic. "We'll go to Vista Mar."

"She might be in danger," I mumbled. Ben didn't know about any of the weird supernatural stuff, as far as I knew. We rode in silence for a time as I tried to figure out how to tell him this truth that would make me sound absolutely insane.

I thought of poor Bud from my discarded short story, who had found himself in a similar situation. I'd never finished the story. I'd never figured out how.

"They aren't what people think they are," I said, a while later, trailing an arm out the window.

"Who?" Ben asked, eyes shifting from the road to me and back.

"Mo. Pirate. Rita. Wyatt Jones. Manny and Señora Chela, Q, all of them. Me. Gran."

"I don't follow," he said. "What does Mo have to do with your boss?" I sighed, propping my elbow on the door, head on my hand. The wind from the open window blew my hair into a tangle I'd regret when we stopped, but the fresh air was a welcome change to Arlo's stuffy apartment. How to explain the impossible?

"Do you believe in . . . magic?"

Ben must have heard something in the tone of my voice because he made a quick right into the exit lane instead of continuing onto the PCH. He pulled into the parking lot of a gas station, cut the engine, and turned to look at me, curious.

"I *knew* there was something out of the ordinary going on," he said. I nodded. "Want to just come out with it? Or do we have to go through . . . a thing?"

I shook my head, not entirely sure. Did I want to come out with it? Or did I need to build up to it so I didn't come across as a person who would benefit from some time in a psychiatric institution? Or prison.

Ben sat back, resting his hands in his lap, relaxed. I watched his eyes follow something through the windshield. A crow with what looked like a string of spaghetti in its beak hopped onto a guardrail in front of Ben's car, then fluttered up into a stunted little tree planted in a patch of dirt at the edge of the lot.

"It's a straw wrapper," Ben said, "she's lining her nest."

"City dwellers make do," I said, remembering the egret standing in the concrete chute that cradled the LA River.

"I saw a couple of ravens fighting over a bag of chips the other day," Ben said. "Nacho cheese. I couldn't help but wonder how junk food affects the digestive systems of corvids."

"Hmm."

"You know, there's a Jewish mysticism tradition, the Kabbalah, that's pretty esoteric," Ben said. "I got interested in it as a teenager. Fascinating stuff. It says, and my gut agrees, that the universe is much more complicated than rational thought is capable of comprehending—and what's magic but that which defies rational explanation, right?" He turned to me. When I met his eyes, they appeared to darken. I did not detect even a hint of skepticism. "Tell me what's on your mind, Queenie."

I told him everything. *Everything.*

"That's a wild story," he said once I'd finished and slumped back in the passenger seat, exhausted. Ben reached over and took my hand and squeezed it. "I believe you."

But did he though? Really?

"We should drive," I said, squeezing back. "I'm worried about Mo."

Back on the road, minutes from Vista Mar, I borrowed Ben's phone to call Gabe García and Dolores Bresson, the agents who had approached me my first day at the restaurant. *We protect people,* Bresson had said. Maybe they could find the people Angelo had essentially sold into slavery. Wyatt probably wouldn't like it, but I was past caring.

García picked up right away. I told him about Angelo, how he'd been smuggling refugees. I didn't mention Wyatt, Rita, and Pirate's more altruistic operation. It was possible they could hide their involvement and simply provide the information the feds would need to track down the missing people.

"Are there migrants there now?" he asked.

"I don't think so. But I know where the secret room is . . . sort of. Isn't that evidence?"

"Not strong enough," he said. "And we'd need a warrant to search it. You have any reason to believe Wyatt knew about all this? You sure he wasn't involved?"

"Not exactly." I took a deep breath, trying to get my thoughts straight. "The guy, Angelo, who was forcing people into a truck at gunpoint, he worked in the kitchen. He's dead."

"Dead?"

"Out on Pirate's boat, with Wyatt and Rita. It was—an accident. He . . . attacked Wyatt."

"His name? Location of the accident?"

I told him as much as I could without revealing that I had jumped overboard and that Wyatt might even think I was dead. The sound of rapid typing came through from García's end. Finally, he said "Here's what you're going to do, Queenie. Go to Vista Mar, now. Pretend you're there to pick up your check, like before. Quit. Tell Wyatt Jones you're not coming back to work. Get your friend if she's there and get out. Agent Bresson and I are on our way over to ask Mr. Jones some questions about the whereabouts of his head chef, so if you run into any trouble, we'll be there to back you up."

"Okay," I said, feeling woozy, fully regretting the call.

"Thanks for calling."

"Yeah."

As I spoke, Ben's eyes flicked from me to the road. He looked, understandably, about as worried as I felt. I knew reporting this might cause trouble for Wyatt and the restaurant. But it was a situation where the ends would justify the means, surely. If they could find those people . . .

"Who exactly did you just call?" Ben asked.

"These agents investigating suspicious activity at the restaurant," I said. "They approached me my first day. Federal agents."

"They'll deport them, you know," Ben said. "They're probably ICE agents."

"What?"

"If they do find those missing, they'll deport them."

I dialed Manny's then. The phone rang for what seemed like forever. He picked up with a tired, "Yup?"

"Manny, it's Queenie."

"Hi, Queenie."

"Mo went looking for me at Wyatt's. I'm worried she's going to run into trouble."

"Queenie?"

"What?"

"You time traveled. Q noticed the ripples in the net. More like goddamn tidal waves. What were you thinking?"

"I needed to find out what happened to Gran," I said. My hand, holding the phone up to my ear, suddenly felt leaden. The feeling of wanting to jump overboard that I'd had on Pirate's boat returned full force. My gaze drifted to the door handle.

"And did you?"

"Not exactly." He drew in a breath. I could tell he was about to give me an earful.

I hung up, then turned the phone off for good measure.

I tossed the phone on the dash and slumped back in my seat. When we pulled into the parking lot, the restaurant appeared mostly deserted. No steam emitted from the fan at the back. Pirate's car and Wyatt's were the only ones visible, but sometimes the cooks parked around the corner, where I couldn't see.

When we entered through the main door, we saw Mo first. She was turned away from us, standing on a slatted patio table, one arm outstretched toward Pirate as if holding him off. Pirate looked like he'd just reeled back against the deck rail. His hands were raised before his face as if in self-defense.

My first instinct was to go to them, but Ben held me back. Mo might have the advantage momentarily, but she was defending herself against a much larger, more physically powerful man.

Ben put a finger to his lips and pointed. As my eyes focused in, I saw a shaft of silver light streaming from Mo's extended hand. I exhaled. A forcefield shimmered around Pirate, holding him in place.

Ben let out a low whistle. Our eyes met and in his, I saw the dawning of real, concrete belief in the impossible. He shook his head. "I thought it was best to play along . . . People imagine strange things sometimes when their loved ones die . . . I thought . . ."

"I know," I said, keeping my voice low. "I get it."

A clatter from the far end of the room nearest the kitchen caught my attention. Maria stood there watching the scene on the patio unfold, a colander dangled from her fingers, a drift of butter lettuce on the floor around her feet, her expression one of total astonishment. I started toward her, weaving silently between the tables. In my haste, I bumped against a fully set table and the shiver of glasses and cutlery sent their high notes singing across the room. Mo looked over her shoulder, scanning the dining room's interior for the source of the noise. I stopped in my tracks, ducked behind the bar instinctively. She turned back to Pirate.

"Where. Is. Queenie?" Mo demanded. "What have you done with her?"

Her face had changed—she was the blood moon, glowing like I'd seen before but her aura tinged red, eyes like embers. Ben gripped my hand tighter.

"I don't know." Pirate spoke with a calm intensity, as one does when trying to appease an enraged animal. "I assumed she would have found her way to you by now."

"What have you done with her?" Mo would not be deflected.

"Nothing! Well, she was with me on the boat. She jumped overboard. But you know that. You helped me save her."

"Did I? I wasn't sure you were going to help her," Mo challenged.

"That girl is learning to help herself," Pirate said. "You hovering over her isn't going to make her strong."

"Wyatt's minion, like always," Mo said, throwing up her hands, which broke the stream of energy she'd been directing at Pirate. "You know, it was nice working together the other night. It really was! It made me see how things could have been all these years, how they might be if Wyatt weren't such a hotheaded maniac and if you and Rita didn't follow along with all he does like a pair of mob henchmen. But I know now I was foolish to hope things could change for the better. Wyatt's got you brainwashed, and you'll never change."

"Minion? Brainwashed?" Pirate wiped sweat from his cheek with the back of his hand. "You should talk. You just go along with what Q says, never questioning or thinking for yourself. Never thinking outside the box. At least Wyatt's not complacent . . . He doesn't sit around waiting for the universe to work itself out, blah blah blah," he mimicked, looking the spitting image of Q. "I believed in Wyatt. Still do!" He stared at Mo defiantly. "Q had no right to interfere with Wyatt and Anke's friendship, and even you could agree we've all suffered the consequences." Beyond him, the high tide surf had worked itself up into ten-foot waves that were breaking so close to the shore I could feel salt spray from where I stood in the dining room. The air crackled around Pirate and Mo, their opposition creating a vortex of energies that I realized were meant to work together. The rift had weakened the guardians for centuries. No wonder the planet was such a mess.

Pirate and Mo had saved me the night I tried to end my life. It did explain how I'd survived. I'd felt so alone when I jumped overboard into the sea, intending to swim until I couldn't swim anymore, until the waves took me. But I hadn't been—I'd been accompanied by the gravitational pull of the moon, its influence on the tides, the interconnected pattern of waxing and waning light, the tide's rise and fall. I'd experienced them moving in a state of cooperation the night they rescued me. Now, witnessing a disturbance in that rhythm, I understood the danger posed by the long-splintered factions of the earth's avatars.

"Hah. Anke was better off without Wyatt's so-called friendship," Mo said. "All his so-called assistance ever did was cause her grief. And here you are, still working for him. He's a murderer! Shame on you, Pirate." Her voice was like knives.

"I would do it all over again," Pirate countered.

"How can you—?" Mo raised her hand again. A stream of light touched Pirate's face making his skin shine as if lit from within. The waves beyond grew even bigger, twisting and turning, crashing against each other with a force that sent seagulls flying up from the beach. Beachgoers, realizing the ocean had suddenly turned dangerous, evacuated the water and retreated up the beach to get away from the erratic surf. Neither of them had noticed those of us watching from the dining room. They were oblivious to all but the fight.

Maria moved to stand beside Ben and me. I looked down as if in a dream, noticing green lettuce leaves from the bowl she'd dropped stuck to the bottoms of her clogs. What could we do to stop this terrible argument? I wondered. Nothing. They were so much stronger than us.

"Bravo!" Wyatt's deep voice crackled from behind us, sending a shiver up my spine. "Very, very good, Mo. You always did put on a good show. We've missed you . . ." He sauntered across the dining room. I hadn't seen him since the boat incident. "I knew you would show up eventually."

The earth began to move in an intense, wavelike rolling motion for what felt like a full minute, sending pictures and plates and glasses and bottles crashing to the floor. The chandelier over the center of the dining room swung, hundreds of crystal pieces making a sound like a hailstorm as they clattered together. Crouched beneath the lip of the bar with Ben and Maria, I watched Wyatt advance slowly across the parquet floor while the world shuddered. Mo, moving just as deliberately, stepped toward him.

"We could do so much if we all worked together," Wyatt said, spreading arms wide, as if inviting Mo and Pirate and the ocean and the sky into an embrace. "Isn't that right, Pirate?" He shook his head. "Too bad we've wasted all this time fighting."

The shaking stilled as the front door opened as if blown by a strong draft. A waft of butter-scented air blew into the dining room. Manny, Señora Chela, and Q strode through the dining room to join the others, almost as if they were expected.

"What's going on?" Maria whispered; her hand gripping my arm was shaking violently. I shook my head. Even with all I knew, I had no explanation for this.

"Where's Rita?" I asked.

"She's been out for a couple days," Maria answered quietly. "Something about a trip to visit relatives in Canada?"

"Should we leave?" I said, wishing I was also in Canada, though not with Rita. I wondered if her trip had anything to do with the group of undocumented refugees. If so, I hoped she was bringing them somewhere safe.

"If we go now, we'll never find out what's going on," Ben said. Maria nodded, wide-eyed. She, of all of us, knew the least about this. I think she was in shock.

"True, but—they're very frightening when they're like this!"

"Queenie," Ben said. "You've got to talk to them. They're your elders. You're one of them."

"I can't do it," I hissed, half standing. I was going to get the fuck out of there if it was the last thing I did. But Ben grabbed the hem of my shirt and pulled me back. "You can help," he said. "Take a breath and get out there. This is ridiculous. If you leave now, you'll regret it forever. Think of your mom. And Gran. Do it for them."

They were all shouting over each other. When I stepped out onto the patio, they fell silent and stared.

"Hi," I said. No one said anything, but they made space for me. "So . . . Earth, Wind, and Fire," I joked feebly. "Like the rock band? Who's fire?"

"Fire is the result of earth and wind coming together, Queenie," Q said, his face serious. "Funny. That's a good one." He did not look like he thought it was funny. I regretted the joke almost as much as I regretted calling Agent García. "You used to be funny, Wyatt," Q resumed the thread of his tirade, throwing up his arms in exasperation. "What did you do with the sweet, hilarious boy I used to know?"

"What did *I* do with him? You must be kidding," Wyatt stormed back. "No, not kidding. You're deranged. See, it's hard to be funny when your people are being enslaved and massacred. And your father, whose job it is to protect them, stands by and does nothing," Wyatt said bitterly. "It's hard to be funny when your own father plots to have you killed."

"Whoever said it was my job to protect the people?" Q replied, throwing up his hands like any frustrated parent whose child fails to acknowledge their sacrifices. "My job is to create, not sustain or protect. I make things and whatever happens is by the will and actions of the people. You know better than anyone, Wyatt, the nature of free will."

"You could have intervened. You could have helped! Instead, you cast me out when the first uprising failed," Wyatt said, studying Q's face. "If it weren't for Pirate, your plot against me would have been fulfilled and all that I have done in service of the people over the past two hundred years would never have been. So where do we find ourselves after doing it your way?" Q looked up but didn't answer. "The native grasses are long gone, smoke from cook fires has been replaced with car exhaust, the hawk scavenges for remains over freeways, and the rivers have been paved and shifted from their natural courses," Wyatt went on. "Are you happy now, Father?"

Q drew himself up to his full height, which was about five foot six, his expression outraged. "Your service?" he sputtered. A touch of the old fire rekindled in his black eyes. The ground gave a warning rumble. Manny put a hand on the old man's arm, whether to guard him or hold him back, I'm not sure. "All you have done is incite failed uprisings and get people killed, Weywot. When you involved Toypurina in the plot at San Gabriel, you robbed the village of a medicine woman with great potential. Imagine what she might have done if she'd been allowed to mature, grow her skills, nurture her gifts. With time, she may have become powerful enough to lead the people to freedom, to reclaim our lands, our villages, our homes."

Wyatt cringed, apparently at the memory.

"I hear you are in the human trafficking business now, Weywot," Q continued, nodding sagely. "Tell me, son, how does the forced exploitation of men, women, and children serve the people?"

"I am not trafficking!" Wyatt roared, his thunder matching that of his father's. The way they were standing, facing each other head-to-head, I could see, for the first time that they were, indeed, related. "I'm a smuggler, yes," he said more quietly, "but I do it to help people—people trying to escape from life-threatening circumstances, not to turn a profit or harm them."

He turned to me. "Queenie, you should know your ICE agents aren't coming."

Uh-oh. I sat on a chair, crossing my arms protectively over my chest.

"Oh, thank god," I breathed. "I shouldn't have called. I realized as soon as I got off the phone . . ."

"It's okay. Gabe and Dolores are with me," Wyatt explained, taking a seat beside me. "You see, I had to test you when you first arrived, find out what you were made of. García and Bresson work inside ICE to keep children with their parents, make sure detained migrants have legal representation, that kind of thing. That means that sometimes they work against the policies of the United States government." He looked up at Q.

"If that's true, then I support you in your work," Q conceded after a pause. "But tell me, how has Queenie become involved in all of this? Anke broke ties with you long ago. I made sure of that."

Instead of answering Q's question, Wyatt turned to me. "It's true," he said. "Queenie is long overdue for an explanation—from all of us," he said, looking around at the assembled guardians. He looked at me intently. "My relationship with your grandmother was more complex than perhaps my father has ever been able to understand," he said, sitting back on the table behind him.

"Were you . . . together?" I asked, the words catching in my throat. I was really asking if Wyatt was my biological grandfather.

"No," Wyatt countered. "Absolutely not. We were just friends. Good friends. But that doesn't mean that our relationship was in her best interest," he said. "I have a reputation as being selfish, impulsive, and willful. This reputation is well-deserved, though I've tried to learn and grow with age. Anke saved me once, from doing something I would have regretted. I lost my temper—on the film set where we met? Flew into a rage. Nearly strangled a . . . cameraman." The last word he spat like it was poison. "She talked me down. Wasn't scared of me at all. Nobody ever did that before. Once I get going everyone usually runs . . . but she helped me."

"I just wanted the best life possible for her and for the child," Q broke in. I wasn't sure what he was talking about. What did Gran's child have to do with the film set?

"The child," I repeated. "You mean my mother, Althea."

I felt, rather than saw, everyone exchange glances.

"Your mother . . ." Wyatt began, then stopped.

Pirate stepped forward and took both my hands. "Queenie," he said, his eyes kind and sad. "When your grandmother was working on that film set, she was . . . assaulted. That was why Wyatt went after the cameraman. He found out what the bastard had done to Anke."

It took a few beats for me to respond. "Are you sure?" Ben came to stand behind me; he rested his hands on my shoulders. Mo kneeled, also bracing me with her hand on my knee. My first thought was of Grandad. "Did my grandfather know?"

Pirate nodded. "She told him, of course. As you know, Cedric considered Althea to be his own."

"So . . . why did Gran stop being friends with Wyatt? And . . . all of you?"

"Anke was pregnant," Pirate said, shrugging. "She'd been fired from her job at Union Station once she started showing. She hadn't told Cedric yet about the baby and wasn't sure she wanted to. He'd been away, working. She was worried how his family would take it, assumed they'd never accept her. She'd stopped trusting people."

Wyatt broke in. "I asked Q to watch out for her."

"Why didn't you just help her yourself?" I asked. "Why drag Q into it?"

"The only income Anke had at that point was from reading cards for passersby. She was getting bigger every day, had no family, wouldn't accept money from me or listen to anything I said." Wyatt shook his head sadly. "She was completely traumatized, unreachable." Wyatt turned his palms to the sky. "I could see her spiraling and I was powerless to stop it. Going to Q was a last resort . . . and I knew he would refuse to get involved unless he thought he was cleaning up another of my messes."

"Humph," Q snorted, crossing his arms over his chest. "So you lied."

"I told him the child was mine," Wyatt admitted. "I knew he was the only one who could help her heal. He promised to help her. But in exchange, I promised to never see her again."

So, Wyatt had gone to his father as a last resort to help Gran, just as Gran had gone to him as a last-ditch attempt to help me. The irony of this took my breath away. History repeats itself sometimes in the strangest of ways.

"A promise you did not keep," Q interjected.

"When your mother got into trouble while she was working as a paralegal at City Hall, Anke contacted me," Wyatt explained, sighing. "I tried to help as best I could. Still am," he said. "She uncovered a corruption plot that ran so deep, the information she discovered put her life in danger. You won't remember, you were too young. But there were threats; some of them quite twisted. She had to leave."

She had to leave. Why didn't she take me?

One thing after another, the mysteries cleared up and more mysteries revealed. First, I found out my mother wasn't Grandad's biological child. That Gran had been raped. Now, the business with my mother. I'd never dared hope she might return because I couldn't bear to be disappointed again. I was gathering the courage to ask: What about my mother? Is she alive? Where is she? when Q slumped into a chair opposite me, weeping.

"I suppose I must admit that perhaps I've made some mistakes," he sobbed. Tears dripped onto his cheeks and slid off his chin into his lap, turning the deep blue fabric of his tunic dark in spots. There was a commotion down on the shore, and we all turned to see a seagull snatch a bag of potato chips from an untended picnic basket. I watched in amazement as it flew toward us and deposited the unopened bag in Q's lap before winging away out over the water. "I am truly sorry," Q said, ripping it open. He met each of our eyes in turn. The rustle of cellophane and the furious crunching of Q's stress-eating momentarily drowned out even the sound of the ocean, as well as my thoughts, for which I was grateful. Then, Señora Chela, who I hadn't noticed leave, returned to the patio holding a stack of papers.

"Ah," she said, observing Q's face wet with tears. "I see I've missed something important." Manny opened his mouth to speak, but she shushed him. "Later." She held up the papers. "Now, the most important thing is the matter of these random earthquakes that have been occurring," she said, turning to Wyatt. "They've been small—so far. But a big one is coming. I can feel it. It might be tomorrow or thirty years from now, but something has been disturbed inside the earth and I need to see if there's any way to . . . redirect the pattern. But to do that, I must know where it's coming from. So, I was thinking . . ." She turned to Wyatt. "Wyatt, forgive me. I went to look in your office because I had an idea about something." She held up the papers. The letterhead on the top page displayed an image I recognized—the logo stamped on the oil rig we'd visited on Pirate's boat.

"Will you break my heart again, Weywot?" Señora Chela asked, looking like it was already broken. "You're working for DRK-Oil?"

"Oh!" Wyatt said. "It's something I've been working on. But it's not what you think. It's—" he glanced at me. "Actually connected with Althea's situation."

Señora Chela sat back on her heels and studied Wyatt for some moments. He met her gaze steadily. "I bought shares in the oil company because I suspected they've been fracking illegally, right offshore," Wyatt continued. "It was part of what Althea discovered—backroom deals and permits. They've been injecting vast quantities of wastewater under the seabed at several sites disguised as oil rigs."

"Ah, well," Señora Chela, said, rising to her feet. "That would certainly explain the earthquakes." She shook the papers in Wyatt's face. "I read in the papers you're a major shareholder for this company?"

"I am," Wyatt said.

"You would stand to lose a good deal of funds if the company is taken to court and found guilty?" she asked.

"I would," Wyatt replied. "A lot of money."

"Good boy," Señora Chela said, breaking into a smile. She bent to hug Wyatt, then touched Q's shoulder. "Brush off your tunic, Quaoar," she said. "You're covered in potato chip crumbles." For a moment, I could see how the three of them were a family, long estranged, reunited.

"As I was saying," Wyatt said, "because of the nature of the information she found, she began receiving death threats that escalated to the point where she was not only worried about her own safety, but yours," he said. "And her parents. That's why we went out on the boat the other day to take those photos, Queenie, of the injection well."

"Jeez," I said.

"Yeah. I have almost enough evidence to construct a rock-solid case against the oil companies, as well as certain politicians and lobbyists, but for one thing . . ."

"What?" I asked, wondering how there could possibly be more to this already very complicated story.

"It will require Althea's testimony," he said.

Eighteen

It was well past dark by the time Ben turned his car into the driveway to drop Mo and me off at the bungalow. We'd gone to the police station for my rescheduled psych evaluation, which Ben arranged over the phone from Vista Mar following the Great Reckoning, as I'd begun half-jokingly referring to the scene on the patio. I wasn't sure how it had gone. When they asked me questions about whether I'd ever been involved in any illegal activities, my heart started beating fast thinking about Rita's gun and Angelo's body disappearing beneath the waves. I was sweating and couldn't stop. But they hadn't arrested me on the spot, which I took as a good sign. The bad sign came when we arrived home.

Illuminated by the streetlights, they were strewn across the front yard, the stoop, the driveway. At first, I couldn't tell what I was looking at, the sight was so bizarre and out of place. More than a dozen black cormorants and seagulls and at least three pelicans in various stages of decomposition. The smell hit me before I got out of the car. We briefly regarded the scene in a collective state of abject horror before running for the kitchen door. Nudging a limp white gull aside with the toe of my sneaker from where it blocked the screen door, I yanked it open. A folded piece of yellow-lined legal paper fluttered to the ground. Ben retrieved it. I managed to unlock the door, and the three of us stumbled into the kitchen. Mo slammed the door shut. Gasping after holding our breath against the sweet, cloying stench of decay, we stared at each other in shock.

"Oh my god," I said, switching on the light. My hands were trembling so hard I could barely hold the teapot under the faucet.

"Who—?" Mo said, raking fingers through her hair. "How—?"

"We have to call the police," Ben said, collapsing into a chair at the table. "There's nothing else to do . . . If someone hasn't already." My gaze drifted to the front window. The grisly scene had not vanished. It was not a nightmare or any kind of figment of my imagination.

"Someone put those there," Mo said. Her face was paper white, but not in her glowing moon way. All the blood had drained from it. Ben's was similar, and I imagined mine was, too.

"Unless... something happened?" I posed unconvincingly. "Like a natural phenomenon?"

"A natural phenomenon occurring only in your yard?" Ben said, shaking his head. "It's a threat, Queenie. A serious threat."

"The paper!" I reminded him, pointing to the yellow paper clasped in his hand. In our fright, we'd forgotten about it. "Whoever did this must have—" As he fumbled to unfold it, I could see Ben was as shaky as I was. I experienced a wave of gratitude that the windows were closed. If I'd caught another whiff of the birds just then, I would have thrown up. Mo took the kettle from me and put it on the stove. Lighting the burner, she reached up for the sugar bowl on the shelf.

"Queenie," she said, "did you move the little doll-thing that you keep extra cash in?"

"No-o-o," I said, turning to look. It was gone. In the place where Gran's Russian doll had sat for as long as I could remember, the one that matched the one in Wyatt's office, was empty space. "Someone was here, oh my god, again. Someone... I—" I put my hands to the sides of my head. I was dizzy and there was a hot pulse behind my eyes that was becoming very disorienting. I couldn't think.

"Who's Damien?" Ben asked, looking up from the yellow paper.

"The asshole neighbor. Why?"

"He... wants to take you out to dinner?"

"What?" I think we'd all been expecting the yellow paper to be about the dead birds. A warning, maybe. Some explanation. Ben waved the note at me. I snatched it out of his hand.

> Queenie—
> I've had some thoughts regarding your predicament. Please allow me to make up for my un-neighborly behavior the other evening by taking you out to dinner. Tomorrow? I was caught off guard.
> Damien

At the bottom of the note was a phone number.

While we waited for the police, we searched the house for further evidence that someone had been in the house while we were gone. The house had been locked when we returned home. There was no sign of a break-in. The matryoshka was missing, and Gran's last remaining journal, which I remembered leaving on my desk.

The yard was cordoned off as a crime scene. I told the officers someone had been in the house. When Detective Barnes showed up, she sat me down and let me know they were still looking into the witnesses who had implicated me in the crime, but that she was also concerned I might be in serious danger and wanted to know if there was any reason I could think of that someone might want to scare me.

"This isn't normal," she said, gesturing to the team photographing the birds outside, dusting for fingerprints inside. "In all my years doing this job... never anything like it."

"But the birds. Where did they—?"

"Poisoned," she said darkly. "Least, that's what it looks like. We'll send samples to the lab to verify."

"Jesus," I said. When she said it, a bitter taste flooded my mouth like I was feeling what the poor creatures had gone through.

"It took some leg work on the part of whoever is responsible," she continued, standing. "They didn't all die at the same time, and they didn't die here. They were brought here from somewhere else and placed around your front yard."

"I have no idea why someone would want to threaten me," I said as I walked her to the door. "Isn't it weird there's no explanation? And the fact that someone's been in the house... more than once. Sorry I didn't tell you about last time."

"Change the locks at the very least." She secured the top button on her trench coat. "We're placing your house under round-the-clock surveillance, but if I were you, I'd find someplace else to stay until we get to the bottom of this."

"Right," I said. "Okay. I'll try to figure something out."

"Once the crew is done, Sanitation will be by to get the rest of the birds. They'll clean it up well, so you won't have to worry about contamination."

"Thanks," I said, holding back tears that were more about the loss of Gran's journal than fear for my safety. The detective patted my arm before she left, which made me hopeful she didn't really believe I could have been involved in Gran's death. I appreciated her concern, but Detective Barnes didn't, and couldn't, know the whole story. Her warnings strengthened my resolve to find Gran's killer myself. All of it was connected, I was sure of it. How could

I expect regular old city cops to solve a crime that was obviously not regular? And while I had come to understand that we avatars were not only fallible, but extremely limited in our powers, I knew I had to stay at the bungalow with Mo. Whoever was doing this knew I was here. They wanted something from me. When they came back, I'd be ready for them.

In the meantime, I wanted to know what Damien was playing at. He knew my name, and I was sure he'd seen me the night Gran died. So why mess with me? Then, a conciliatory note stuck in my door the same day a bunch of dead birds were planted in my yard. Something was not quite right about that man. I decided I would accept his dinner invitation and find out what exactly what his deal was.

Ben didn't want to leave us alone, so we moved Mo's things into Gran's room. We opened the windows and put fresh sheets on the bed. I'd spent no more than a few seconds in her room since she died. When I opened her closet, a rush of sandalwood rose from her clothes and washed over me. I ran a hand over her dresses and jackets, remembering what it felt like to rest my cheek on her shoulder, to breathe in her comforting scent. There was a corner of paper sticking out of the pocket of her navy blazer. Gingerly, with the uneasy sensation I was prying into her private business, I pulled it free. It was a flyer for a community meeting about the housing development in the wetlands. Anke Rivers was listed on the agenda as a speaker. Four other names were cited.

One of them was Damien Drucker, on behalf of CC Residential. The date of the meeting was set for the day after Gran was killed.

Nineteen

As soon as City Sanitation cleared the dead seabirds away, I called Damien. I didn't say anything about what had happened at the bungalow the night before, and he didn't ask. We agreed he would make reservations at Vista Mar for that evening.

"You think we can trust Wyatt and Pirate and Rita, that they'll have your back?" Mo asked.

I shrugged. "I hope so. I have to believe what they've been doing amounts to . . . family drama. That they aren't killers."

"We know they are. Or Rita is, anyway. She killed Angelo. We should figure out another way to do this," Ben said from the bathroom doorway.

"Angelo was selling people into slavery," Mo reasoned, "and he threatened Wyatt. It was self-defense."

"No time for an alternate plan," I said, applying mascara.

"Are you absolutely sure?" Mo asked again, passing me a tube of lipstick. "Maybe we should call the restaurant and fill them in."

"Too complicated," Ben said. "And what if they're not innocent—we don't know for sure they weren't involved."

"I'm only going to ask once more . . ." Mo said.

"Yes," I said. "I'm sure. I'm going. He's the murderer. He could easily have been the dark shape walking up the road after Gran threw Rita out. I suppose it's possible she was involved somehow . . . It's all connected. I don't know exactly . . . But I'm going to find out if it kills me."

To which Ben replied, "Queenie, just don't."

"Don't what?" I asked.

"Don't get killed."

To which I replied, "Shut up or I'll cry and we'll have to do this stupid makeup all over again."

Mo took the brush from me and pulled my hair back into a ponytail. Watching her serene, beautiful face concentrate on the task in the bathroom mirror, aware of Ben's grounding presence in the doorway, I was struck by the realization that amidst the horror and chaos, I'd managed to make two very dear friends. For a moment, I was filled with gratitude.

Damien picked me up in his black sedan at seven on the dot, like he said he would. I wore steel-toed motorcycle boots and a studded leather jacket with a can of pepper spray in one pocket and my cell with my location shared and Ben's number queued on speed dial in the other. He and Mo's plan was to stay at the house and wait for my call. They were ready to alert Detective Barnes if there was so much as a single ring from my number.

The conversation was quite awkward. He was driving, looking from me to the road, explaining how when I mentioned the murder, asking him to talk to the detectives, it made him very nervous because he was new to town, trying to prove himself at his new job, and didn't want to get involved in anything untoward (yes, he used that word). I watched him while he spoke, trying to read his body language and expression. The more I listened, the more I became convinced that he was the murderer. Which meant I was in danger, and I couldn't afford to provoke his anger in a situation without backup by asking questions, though I was dying to ask about his connection to the residential developers, and the hearing. And whether or not he knew Gran. And why he had killed her.

"Let's get one thing straight," I said when he'd screeched to a halt just in time at a red light. My voice sounded much more confident than I felt.

"What?" he asked, looking at me. I noticed his pupils seemed dilated and wondered if he was on something.

"I work at Vista Mar. You may not do anything to embarrass me." I said it lightly.

"Oh shit, you work there?" he said, breaking into loud laughter that resulted in spit flying from his mouth and landing in my eye. "And here I just thought you fancied yourself a classy date when you asked me to book there." I blinked and wiped my face, feeling sullied.

"Just try and get us there in one piece, okay?" I sat back in my seat and fingered the pepper spray in my pocket, imagining how if he tried anything I'd aim for his eyes, pull up the lock, and jump out of the car. I knew this city well, and he was a stranger here. I had the advantage, or I would once we got to Vista Mar.

It was busy when we arrived. Rita didn't bat an eyelash when she saw me, only greeted us, saying, "Good evening, Queenie," and, "Mr. Drucker, your table is ready for you." I waved to Pirate, who looked me up and down with a raised brow but didn't break his shake-and-pour rhythm to find out what I was doing there. Rita led us to a table in the farthest corner of the dining room from the bar with a view of the piano.

"So," Damien said, unfolding his napkin. "What's good?"

"Crow," I said.

"Excuse me?"

"The roe? You know, fish eggs. For an appetizer. It comes with this beautiful little marinated frisée and cucumber salad with a black sesame reduction drizzled over the top."

"Ah, okay."

When Connor came over to take our order, I asked him to let Wyatt know I needed to talk to him privately before I left.

"How long have you worked here?" Damien asked once Connor moved on.

"Only about a month."

"Nice place."

"Yep."

"Ever think of getting out of the waitressing biz?"

"Does anyone ever seriously think of getting into it? All people who work in restaurants ever do is think about getting out of—the biz—as you put it. No matter if they're an owner, an executive chef, or a dishwasher. Even when we love it, we think constantly about getting out of it."

"I was just thinking, you seem like a sharp lady. And I wondered if you might be interested in trying out a career in PR, you know, public relations," he said, pouring us both more wine from the bottle of red Connor had brought over. Yes, Damien, I know what PR is.

"Interesting," I said, taking a teensy sip from my glass. Indeed, I was sharp, sharper than Damien, anyway; he was definitely on something. And it was an interesting suggestion, but not for the reasons he meant. "So nice of you to think of me. That's what you do, right? I'd love to hear more about your work." I forced a wide smile.

"Sure thing. So I work in PR, for a development firm. CC Residential"

"Wow," I said. "So fascinating. So how's everything going with the Hughes land?"

"Great. Well, mostly great," he said, leaning back in his chair. "That's what I wanted to ask you about. We've run into a small hiccup with some old bones the excavators dug up down at the base of the bluffs. Nothing major. They're just old Indian bones—uh, I mean Native Americans. And some pots and things. But some of these preservationist types are kicking up a fuss, and I was wondering if you might consider pitching in. Since you're local and all and . . ."

"And since my grandmother was a lead organizer in the campaign against development?" I filled in.

Did I imagine a crack forming in his cool, collected veneer? Or was he slightly shaken that I'd put two and two together?

"I am so sorry about your grandmother," Damien said a little too quickly. "See, the other day—I didn't make the connection. I hadn't heard the news about Mrs. Rivers yet. Such a tragedy," he said, shaking his head as if he knew something of sorrow. Then he looked up, his eyes soft, innocent. How did he do that? His expression was so convincing, so endearing, like a puppy. An evil puppy. "I did have the pleasure of meeting her a number of times," he continued. "Even though she was on the opposing side of the controversy, she was a wonderful woman to work with." Damien pushed his plate aside and sat forward, folding his hands together on the table like a judge. "You must be going through such a tough time," he continued. "And with money? I mean, you must need a steady source of income. And we would pay you very, very well." My throat clutched. I felt I couldn't breathe for a second as what he was saying sunk in. He was offering me a job to work against the cause Gran had fought for so passionately. What kind of shallow, idiotic monster did he take me for? I fought the wave of indignation and fury, careful not to let anything show on my face.

"Wow, what an offer," I managed to say. "Um. I do need money. What exactly would I be doing?"

Damien smiled warmly. I hadn't reacted with appalled disgust as any normal person would have in my situation. He thought he had me.

"You'd be my assistant," he said. "You'd speak at meetings, making a case for the economic benefits of the development, talk up the affordable housing we're including, and help negotiate on some environmental points that we are prepared to concede to make it all appear responsible." I must have made a face at this because he fumbled then. "—I mean, it will be responsible. CC Residential is committed to upholding the historical and ecological integrity of the land, above all."

"I don't know what to say," I said distractedly, because inside my head a voice was screaming: hedidithedidithesthefuckingmurdererandyouareouttodinnerwithhimwhatthefuck!

The piano player started up just then. We had a few piano players who came regularly on a schedule, and it was Ricardo's night. Moonlight Sonata infused the warm, bustling atmosphere with that dreamy quality that makes you yearn for more no matter how much good you have in your life. Or how much bad. Oh my god. The besuited neighbor. The dark figure I'd seen walking up the street in my time travel vision. It had to be him. Never mind me needing an alibi for the night in question. It seemed so obvious now, that he'd been there that night, alone. That he saw me leave and took the opportunity to . . .

But I couldn't react. He thought he had me under his control, that I was too dumb to figure out it was him all along. And the birds? He must have done that, too. What a sicko! I had to get a confession. But how? He'd never admit to killing Gran, no matter how stupid and gullible he thought I might be. To calm my nerves, I took a large swallow of wine. Damien refilled my glass.

Ricardo was playing a piece from Vivaldi's Four Seasons. I felt like I was inside it. Nothing mattered except the next right note. It bore me up, but some other force struggled against the strengthening influence of the music. *Focus, Queenie.*

Could I be this tipsy already? Or was it that strange dizzy thing I'd been having? Damien was staring at me intently from across the table. Was I hallucinating or were his pupils expanding and contracting to the rhythm of the piano? And what was the thread of conversation I . . . dropped . . . ?

"Queenie." I looked up to see Wyatt standing beside our table. I hadn't even noticed him approach. "Care to introduce me to your guest?"

"This is . . ." I waved absently toward Damien. "My neighbor."

"I am so sorry to interrupt," he said, taking me by the elbow, helping me rise to my feet. "I must steal Queenie from you for just a minute. Very nice to meet you—?" He looked at Damien questioningly.

"Damien. Damien Drucker. Actually, Mr. Jones, we met a couple of weeks ago. I was here with Bill Collins from the District Attorney's office."

"Ah. I knew you appeared familiar," Wyatt said, blank-faced. He shook Damien's hand with his free one. "We'll be back in a jiff. Just have to go over some paperwork real quick."

"But I have to—" I knew I had to accomplish something that had to do with Damien, but I couldn't for the life of me remember what.

Wyatt steered me through the dining room, up the stairs, to his office. Once I was seated by the open window facing the sea, he gave me the pint glass of ice water Pirate had handed him as we passed by the bar on our way up to the office. He had to wrap both of my hands around it so it wouldn't slip, I was so out of it. Drinking it down, I felt my faculties returning as if one by one. Vision. Touch. Thought. Speech. The ability to form a coherent thought, to speak a full sentence not made up of garbled words, to focus my eyes on what was in front of me.

"What's going on, Queenie?"

"I don't—I don't know." I carefully put the glass down on the coffee table and rubbed my face with both hands, not caring if I smudged my makeup. I took a deep breath. The events of the evening were coming back to me, but slowly.

"I came out to dinner with Damien."

"Yes, he's your neighbor."

"Yes. But. It's more than that."

"You're dating?"

"No!"

"What? You seem out of it."

I looked up. "This has been happening lately... I don't know—" I caught sight of the Russian nesting doll on the shelf, illuminated by the yellow glow of a sconce above it. The doll. The break-in. The fresh air was clearing my thoughts, but not as quickly as I needed. Trying to parse through them felt like looking for lost items in mud. "That doll," I pointed. Wyatt stood and walked across the room to retrieve it.

"Yes," he said. "This doll."

"What does it mean?"

He removed the top and angled it so I could peer into the bottom of the hollow doll. Written in black ink on the rough wood was a number. Or, rather, three numbers.

"These numbers are half of the code for a safe deposit box," Wyatt said. "Inside the box are documents with information about Althea's assumed identity, and her whereabouts." He put the top back on, pressing it between his palms for a moment. "We decided neither of us should know that information, for everyone's protection. We arranged it all through anonymous channels, gave Althea her papers without looking at them ourselves. But we wanted to make sure there was a way for us to get in touch when it became safe. Or in case of an emergency. So, we sealed the information and set up the box. The other half of the code is in Anke's doll." He sat down beside me. I reached out for the doll, and he handed it over. "I've been meaning to ask you to bring it in. So that we can start the process of finding your mother," he said, smiling. Then he noticed my dismayed expression. "What's the matter?"

"It's gone," I moaned, leaning my elbows on my knees and dropping my head in my hands. "Someone broke in yesterday and took it and—" I sat bolt upright, remembering. "They put dead birds in my yard. And that guy. Damien. The one downstairs?" Wyatt nodded. My throat contracted as a dark emotion I couldn't name welled up inside me. "I think he killed Gran."

"Explain," Wyatt said. He glanced at the door like his first instinct was to immediately go after Damien but thought better of it. As I contemplated how to formulate my explanation, the thing that had been nagging at me, that I hadn't shared with anyone, shifted to the forefront of my mind as if nudged by an instinct in me that was wiser than my rational thoughts. I hadn't told anyone about time traveling; seeing me or someone impersonating me entering the house while I was sure that actual me was still on a walk with Daisy, because part of me was afraid it *was* me. Small shreds of shame hung around the memory like the loose feathers Sanitation had so painstakingly removed from my yard.

"First—there's something that's been bothering me," I said, and it already felt like a confession. Wyatt nodded, encouraging me to go on. The rest came out in a rush. Wyatt listened, silent, though his expression betrayed his discomfort.

"I must come clean about something," he said when I was done. I'd thought I'd figured out who I could trust. Now I wasn't so sure. I looked at the one exit, feeling trapped, as Wyatt stood between me and the door. I remembered the pepper spray in my pocket and my phone. "A few things," Wyatt continued. My apprehension ratcheted up a few more notches. I put my hands in my pockets and braced myself. "When Anke called about giving you a job, the timing was perfect. I asked her for the rest of the code, but she wouldn't give it to me. Said her family had suffered enough, and I should go ahead without bothering Althea." Wyatt shrugged guiltily. "I didn't agree, so I sent Rita to your grandmother's house the day you interviewed for the job here. I asked her to get the doll. We were so close to having everything we needed for a hearing, but I knew we'd need to find Althea and convince her to testify to make it stick. Rita, being a shapeshifter, thought the easiest way to do it would be to pretend to be you, but Anke didn't buy it." I remembered Gran kicking me/Rita out the front door, experiencing a surge of pride.

"The other break-ins?" I asked. "Was that you? Why didn't you just ask me for it?"

"I was planning to," Wyatt said, looking confused. "We talked about this the other day, Queenie, when everyone was here. Other break-ins?"

"Yes! Since that night, someone's been in my house at least twice. The first time they broke the lock on Gran's trunk and took her journals. The second time, though, they didn't even break-in . . ." A thought was dawning on me. "Oh my god, they have a key!" I thought back to the night I'd arrived home sans house key when Randy was there. Had someone gone into my locker and taken it off the ring while I was working? My mind was running at top speed, and it looked like Wyatt's was, too. The first break-in, whoever it was, had stolen the journals but not the doll, which didn't make sense. Except—of course—I'd tucked it away under the sink in my fog after Gran was killed as it held the cash that had to last me until I saved up some money from Vista. Little did I know at the time, it held something far more valuable than money. I'd only been half-afraid of someone breaking in again and stealing it. Once I'd amassed enough tips to take it to the bank, the doll had become, once again, a vessel for spare change, and it had resumed its place on the shelf.

"You think Rita broke in those other times? Looking for the doll?"

Wyatt shook his head. "I told her to back off, that we'd wait and see how things went with you . . ."

"The journals?"

"The only thing I can think of is that someone—Rita?—might think the journals could contain information about Althea's location. But why would Rita . . ."

"Unless Rita wasn't working for you," I said, pieces coming together quickly the way a puzzle does when it's near the end. Wyatt, who'd been studying the doll I'd given back to him in bewilderment, looked up, eyes wide as if he'd been struck. "What if Rita wanted to find Althea for some other reason—or some other person?"

"No," Wyatt said, shaking his head, denial in the set of his jaw. "Rita's loyal. It doesn't make sense."

"Think of it," I said. "Rita encounters all the people you do here. She meets the city councilors and sheriffs and CEOs." I leaned in and spoke in a low voice, just in case someone (Rita) was listening outside the door. "Damien was here before with Bill Collins from the DA's office."

"Yes, I know Bill . . ."

"Damien works for CC Residential but was taken out to dinner by Bill Collins. Does that make sense?"

"Not unless—"

"Unless someone in the DA's office has an interest in the development of the Hughes property." I grasped his hand. "Wyatt, I'm almost positive Damien killed Gran. But why would some random PR guy from Portland do something like that?" The memory of Rita holding the gun after she killed Angelo popped into my head. At the time, I was too shocked to give her expression much thought. But now I remembered she hadn't looked sorry at all, or upset. She just looked . . . nothing. Like shooting him didn't bother her one bit.

"He would do something like that if . . . if a powerful person told him to. And that person would only give an order like that if they were afraid she had information that would hurt him . . . and if she had threatened to expose it. Oh no, Althea! It's got to be the same person Althea dug up all the dirt on!"

"Gran was scheduled to speak out against the development *the next day*."

"But Rita didn't take your doll—"

"She wouldn't have to!" I sputtered. "She's got eyes, doesn't she? And a pen!"

We looked at each other. The dawning of comprehension flooded Wyatt's features, then his expression darkened. In unison, we turned to the door and raced downstairs.

I pressed the number one on my phone to call Ben as we dashed downstairs. At the bottom, I tugged Wyatt's shirt, stopping him. "The location of the safe deposit box," I demanded, pointing to the phone at my ear. "Quickly!" He rattled off the address, took a breath to compose himself, then proceeded briskly into the dining room. I stayed crouching in the stairwell. Ben picked up and I launched into an explanation, keeping it as brief as possible. I gave him a description of both Damien and Rita, and the address and number of the lockbox. I asked him to call Detective Barnes and get her over there. "Damien killed Gran," I hissed. "Rita's in on it too."

But then the door, which I'd been leaning against, burst open, causing me to sprawl onto the carpet. The back of my head smacked hard against the host station. Rita leaped over my prone body and bounded up the stairs, taking them two at a time. By the time I struggled to my feet, she was back with a folder of papers I recognized—the one with the logo of one of the oil companies on the front. Wyatt's evidence. I moved to block her. She slammed into me so hard my breath left me. I doubled over, gasping. I wrestled the heavy front door open and staggered out into the parking lot in time to see Wyatt and Pirate running at top speed after Damien's despicable black sedan as it peeled out of the parking lot.

Twenty

We left Vista Mar in the understaffed yet capable hands of Connor and the other servers, and of course Maria and the other cooks. Not usually given to prayer, all I could do as we sped down the PCH in Pirate's car was pray that Detective Barnes would listen to Ben and show up at the safe deposit box store in time to apprehend Damien and Rita.

The storefront in Beverly Hills was nondescript. No sign of Damien's black sedan. Nor was there a cop car in sight.

"Don't stop," I said, leaning forward from the back seat to peer between Wyatt and Pirate through the windshield. "Drive around the corner in case they're watching."

We parked on a side street and got out.

As soon as we turned the corner, the street erupted with the wail of sirens, flashing lights, and uniformed officers brandishing firearms. Trouble was, the weapons were pointed at us. We all three put our hands up.

"Don't move," came the command, like at the climax of a cop movie when the suspects are finally apprehended. Except the voice was familiar. And we weren't suspects. Well, I was. But surely not anymore if Ben had filled the detective in on recent developments? I blinked against the glare of headlights to make out Detective Barnes leaning against an unmarked car in her trench coat, notepad and pen poised. Beside her stood another person I recognized. It was my old pal, Sheriff Melvin Toro. *You new here, sweetheart?*

"You're all under arrest for the suspected murder of Angelo Cipriani," she said, gesturing for her crew to move forward with handcuffs.

"There's been a misunderstanding," Wyatt said as an officer secured his hands behind his back.

"Wyatt Jones!" Melvin Toro exclaimed, apparently taken aback when he recognized him. "Fancy seeing you here. Well, I'm sure this is a big mix-up and we'll all get it sorted out," he said, chuckling. Nervously, I thought.

"What are you doing here, Toro?" Wyatt asked.

"Got called in on account of a report that a formerly incarcerated individual has gone missing, allegations of murder." He glanced at Detective Barnes. "Angelo Cipriani."

"Where's Damien Drucker?" I shrieked, losing my cool. "And Rita!" Pirate, who had been shoved up against a squad car by three officers, quite unnecessarily as he wasn't struggling at all, shot me a look over his shoulder clearly meant to warn me to shut my mouth.

Sheriff Toro eased his back off the unmarked car and advanced toward me in one smooth motion, reminding me of those charmed snakes that dance to the music of a flute. "Mr. Drucker has been taken in for questioning." His speech was as slick as his movement. "I understand you have concerns about him accessing a lockbox that doesn't belong to him. Or so my colleague gathered from your lawyer friend. What was his name? A Mr. Benjamin Schwartz?"

"That's right," I said, feeling the cold cuffs fasten around my wrists. "I hope you handcuffed him, too?"

"Well, you'll be relieved to know we intercepted him before he entered the store. I hope that sets your mind at ease."

Yes, ease is exactly what I was feeling. Thank you, Sheriff Toro, I thought sarcastically. Out loud: "Why are we being arrested? We didn't kill anyone." It was true. "Damien Drucker killed my grandmother. I know if you search his house and compare it with the evidence gathered at the scene of the murder, you'll see I'm right."

"All in due course," he said, "all in due course." And then he had the nerve to pat my arm.

"What about Rita?" I asked, aiming the question at Detective Barnes, who was writing away in her notebook.

She looked up, regarding me neutrally through her tortoiseshell frames. "Damien Drucker was alone," she said, pushing the glasses up her nose. "I don't know anything about a Rita."

"I wonder if this 'Rita' even exists," Toro laughed, forming mocking air quotes around her name with his fingers.

Well, fuck, I thought, as we were put in three separate cars and hauled down to the station.

The questioning went on all night. In the beginning we were interrogated separately, then, once they realized we really had something on Gran's murder, they brought us into a room together. Officers were dispatched to gather documents and testimony from various places and people, including Vista Mar, the bungalow, Damien's house, and even Manny's mercadito. Later, we learned that Damien called his boss from the road. Not the high-up boss (the anonymous one we all knew existed but couldn't name, who no one could touch) but Bill Collins in the DA's office who, of course, was a buddy of Sheriff Toro's. It all seemed touch and go there for a while. But slowly, point by point, we shot down all allegations against us and built up the case against Damien Drucker. Angelo's body had not been found. Our arrest was based on a missing persons statement filed by Rita (ironic since *she* had actually killed him)—who had disappeared. And the accusation didn't hold up to our unified and consistent denial of involvement with Angelo's alleged disappearance. As all the guardians had collectively agreed that day at Vista, the day of Reckoning, Angelo had quit suddenly (the day before he died, ahem) and left without informing anyone of his plans. As far as anyone knew, he could be in Mexico, or Timbuktu. All's fair in love and war. And this was a case of both. We fought well together, the three of us. I think we would have made Gran and Grandad proud.

The Pacific hems the coast in a state of constant reprise. This vast body of water gives, takes, blusters, and cavorts. At times it is a sheet of glass, others it is a frothing demon. Mostly, it is somewhere in between. Persistent in its presence, even looming, it provides a reflection of most humans insofar as its depths remain as unexplored as our own deepest fears and desires. We stare out to sea in search of answers, and it responds with a constant, ceaseless rush. Vista Mar faces the sea, privileged with an unencumbered sea view. The sea itself doesn't judge, but we who face it learn to consider that people do things for reasons. Called reasons—stemming from our pasts as well as our hopes and dreams—when they fall above a certain moral high watermark. But once they drop below that mark into the realm of what harms, reasons become motives. Everyone harms at some point, and everyone has motives. But not everyone is caught red-handed trying to open a lockbox after murdering an old woman because she believed in and fought for a better world than the one she lived in. This is all to say, I don't know why people do evil things. Some people who are wounded learn to channel their pain into positive action. Some people who are scarred by life for whatever reason are consumed by darkness.

I don't know what made Damien the monster he was. All I know is that he was the tip of an iceberg in a city with more than its fair share of icebergs.

Thanks to photos of footprints that match his shoes, confirming that he entered the bungalow through the front yard prior to Gran's murder, and traces of feather and poison in his otherwise immaculate house, he will likely go to prison. However, there is no hard evidence to implicate anyone in the DA's office or employees of the development firm, only conjecture and coincidence. Rita, having escaped with Wyatt's documents, ensured that our case against corruption in city government—connecting elected city officials not only to illegal activities on the parts of big oil, but also developers, as well as illegal use of funds, etc.—is not imminent. But it's also not all lost. She, and whoever she was working for, didn't get to Althea's information. Nor did they get their paws on Gran's journals. Turns out we were wrong about the first break-in following Gran's death. It wasn't Rita who came into the house the day the journals were taken. It was Pirate. He overheard her discussing "Anke's papers" on the phone one day at the restaurant when she thought the music loud enough to cover her words. When he asked her about it, she deflected, which made him suspicious. Not wanting to rock the boat, he decided to keep an eye on her, and in the meantime, quietly retrieve Anke's papers and store them in a safe place. I punched him on the shoulder when he confessed to this, which seemed to bother him no more than a fly might. He waved me away.

"So, it was you who left the dirt in the carpet in the hallway?" I asked, remembering the day I noticed his boots caked with dirt while I was stocking the bar fridge that day that he came in to work late. "I'm glad it was you and not Rita, lurking around my house while I was in the shower!"

"You've got a hell of a voice, Queenie," he replied. "You should sing more often."

And then, I did something I'd been secretly wanting to do since the moment I first laid eyes on him—I stood on tiptoes and flung my arms around his neck, then I pulled back to stare into his eyes. Pirate had had my back at every turn, whether I realized it at the time or not. I wanted to kiss him.

He thought otherwise.

Pirate turned so my lips landed just south of his right shoulder. He wrapped his arms around me in a bear hug, leaned the side of his head into mine. "Pick on someone your own age, Queenie," he said.

"You're like, thirty-eight or forty?" I said. His laugh reverberated through both our bodies, and I couldn't remember the last time I'd felt so safe, so held.

"You having a crush on me is like having a crush on your doctor," he said. "Or a firefighter that pulled you from a burning building. It's situational, Queenie, you've been through hell . . . It will pass."

"Yeah," I murmured, my face still buried in his shoulder. I didn't even feel embarrassed—just relieved I had made a move, and that he had refused me. It was just another instance of Pirate watching out for me.

"It's just life. All of these feelings, they're part of the story you're telling yourself as you try to make sense of it."

"So, you think I'm confused," I said, pulling back to see his face.

"You're grieving," he answered.

"Yes, I am . . ."

"And not just for your grandmother," he continued, "but for who you were before she died, and you before the accident—"

"How'd you know about the accident?"

"And you before your mom left. Before that, the you before you were born. We all grieve for who we were before we were born."

"That makes no sense," I said, annoyed and comforted at once. It was a strange, unbalanced sensation, like bouncing up and down on one foot to get water out of your ear after swimming.

"Exactly," he said. "And so on and so forth."

"I just feel so lost," I said, picking a fleck of what looked like dried seaweed off his shirt, which smelled of salt wind, the citrus zest he prepared for the bar, and a touch of that swampy smell every bar has that reminds you of every hangover you've ever endured. He grasped my shoulders, holding me at arm's length like Gran used to do when she wanted to give me a good talking to.

"We're all lost, and also not," he said. "This is your story, Queenie. You're a writer, right? The difference between a plot dragging a character along behind it and a character doing what they need to do is the difference between a good story and a bad one. Just make your story a good one."

"Sure," I said. "I'll try."

"Don't try. Just do it."

"Okay! Now you're really reminding me of Gran . . ."

"Good," he said, a wide grin spreading across his face.

"I used to drive her crazy with questions when I was like, eight or nine. She'd do her best answering them all and then snap at me to shut my trap, but it never felt mean. Once I asked her where waves come from, and could they ever stop? She said waves aren't water moving so much as energy moving through water."

"They say the apple doesn't fall far from the tree," Pirate answered, brushing at my shoulders briskly a few times with his palms. It felt like he was sweeping heartache right down my arms and out the tips of my fingers. "Unless someone picks it, packs it in a crate with a bunch of other apples and ships it to some faraway city where people like their apples out of season, in the car with the windows down, and they throw out the core and a crow or a rat eats it from the side of the road, shits out the seeds in a meadow somewhere and a new tree grows. See, the thing about apple trees is they don't reproduce true to type from seed, so a Honeycrisp or a Pink Lady or an Arkansas Black seed makes a new kind of tree, one that doesn't have a known name, can't be labeled as one kind of apple or another. It's not simply a reproduction, but a transformation. Yet it carries something essential with it from the original tree."

"Now you're just talking nonsense," I said, my eyes filling with tears as the scent of apples, somehow, filled the air around us. "I love you, Pirate," I said. "You're a bizarre man." I put my head back on his shoulder and we stood there for some time.

"So are you," he replied after a long pause. "So are you—Anyway," he continued. "I suspect you've been developing actual feelings for someone else. Am I wrong?" I thought of Mo and Ben, how we'd all become so close, how they felt like family—a found family, one I had chosen for myself, and they had chosen me back. Pirate was right. There were times when I'd felt attracted to each of them. One more than the other? I couldn't say. I hadn't investigated the feelings at all. Hadn't thought about it beyond a few sparks here and there. I loved and appreciated them both, was just grateful they were in my life. Truth was, I wasn't ready for romance. I had to learn to be me first.

Wyatt closed the restaurant for a few days after that. A time-out was in order. One night, he invited everyone to his home in the hills. Tucked away up in the canyon, the house was a rustic affair with a wide front porch and a view of mostly sky. In the distance, the sea. When Mo, Ben, and I arrived about an hour before sunset, the reddish clay of the low house was bathed in gold. The smell of sun-toasted sage and grasses and woodsmoke hung in the still air.

Pirate greeted us in the drive and showed us into an interior courtyard where Wyatt had a wood-fired grill going. Fennel, squash, carrots, potatoes, and spring onions were heaped on a platter, ready to be placed over the flames. Inside, the house opened on a high-ceilinged great room of honey-colored wood and lots of windows. A massive woodstove was at the center, surrounded by Turkish-patterned carpets and comfortable-looking couches and chairs.

Manny, Q, and Señora Chela arrived a few minutes after us, loaded down with groceries. Together, we prepared dinner. At once memorial, victory meal, reconciliation gathering, and planning session, the mood was solemnly festive—we had achieved a measure of justice for Gran. We'd fought and won one battle. More loomed on the horizon. Despite my mixed emotions, something in me, some part of me that had been, for as long as I could remember, indistinct, had coalesced. I had realized a center of gravity in me that was independent of anyone or anything outside myself. Also, for the first time, I felt like I belonged.

When the food was ready, the long trestle table held bottles of red wine, carafes of spring water, salads of greens, sliced fruits, shaved roots, and cheeses; each one different, dressed in lemon juice and olive oil. There was the platter of grilled vegetables with rosemary and flaky sea salt, a tureen of mussels cooked in white wine and garlic, platters of dates, currants, and goat cheese, and four whole grilled fish dotted with browned lemon slices. Señora Chela had made several golden loaves of bread that released clouds of fragrant steam when I cut into them.

"A toast," Wyatt said, raising his glass once we were all seated. He looked around, making eye contact with each of us in turn. "Thank you." Q had tears in his eyes as he drank. *The feud is mended*, I thought, dipping a piece of crusty bread in my shallow bowl of mussels and broth, the bright tang of the wine balancing the garlic and the rich, rank, delectable sea creatures. *For now, anyway.* The warmth of the food and drink gradually spread from my belly outward until my body felt like it was humming in tune with the glow of my most pleasant surroundings. Later, a small fire was kindled in a ring of stones in the courtyard. Reclined on a chaise, I looked up to the sky where the smoke appeared to mingle with stars. Manny crouched by the fire, flames illuminating the roots of datura as he sliced into thin rounds and tossed them in a cast-iron pot of boiling liquid. The light danced over the ends of his black hair, casting shadows on the planes of his face. I swear I felt a pulse beneath me that matched the shivering points of light in the sky. Q mumbled something under his breath, a song or a chant, as he fed bits of dried plants and twigs into the fire, first offering bits to the sky, then to the earth. Daisy had wedged herself onto the chair between my legs, her sleeping warmth welcome.

Manny handed me a steaming cup that smelled of earth and green and socks left in a gym bag overnight. I drank one sip, coughing at the bitter taste. Then another, and I lay back again. Closed my eyes.

The still air separates into a dancing mist of almost human forms, shades that leap and swirl against the sky. The weight of Gran's pendant rests heavy and cool on my chest, but when I press my fingers to the stone itself, it's warm.

"Anyone can work for the land, Queenie," Q says aloud. Or maybe his voice is only in my head. Or around it. Or maybe it's something I heard once and am remembering. Or maybe . . . we change as the land and its people shift and change. The elements are unchanging. We're all fragments, each piece a part of something too large and complex to comprehend. I try to sit up to ask a question, holding up a hand to shield my eyes, but now the fire seems too bright to look at and the stars are pinpricks that hurt. I have the sensation of sliding down a slope, unable to stop. I see my body as if from a distance, and it's not unpleasant. The sky is a vaulted ceiling painted over with frescoes of my loved ones stretching across the expanse between me and some other place. Reaching out for them, I long to touch flesh but there is only mist. And I ache to belong to it, this thing that has no end. And I must, but it's also so far beyond me all I can do is observe with amazement. Stories fall from the sky, so many, like words dripping out of the pages of a book. All life, dominoes stretched behind and before me in a wild, swirling pattern extending in all directions. When each one falls is a matter of time, but what is time?

Twenty-One

"First things first," Q grumbled over the steaming rim of his coffee mug the next morning. My head was pounding, and I really didn't want to hear about anything but eggs. Nevertheless, he went on. "There's a hearing with DRK-Oil and the Coastal Commission scheduled. We need to submit Wyatt's evidence and make sure this goes to trial. Also, Damien's arrest has triggered an investigation into CC Residential and its connections to City Hall. Before we left the city, Wyatt arranged to contact a very important potential witness."

"It ties together Anke's death, the oil company, *and* Angelo's trafficking," Wyatt said. "Whether any of it goes anywhere will depend on you, Queenie."

"What could I possibly do?" I asked, taking a sip of my coffee. It went down the wrong way and I choked, setting my cup down on the patio table while Pirate patted my back.

"The oil stuff goes way back . . . This potential witness has been living in hiding in the mountains in France for the last twenty-six years," Pirate said.

Twenty-six years. That would have been 1984. Nine years before Grandad had his fatal heart attack. The year I turned five. The year Althea disappeared.

Señora Chela leaned over, put her hands on my shoulders. I could feel their warmth through my thin sweater. She smelled of coffee and buttered toast. "Queenie," she said, "as you probably guessed, the witness is your mother. All those years ago, she dug up information that could get a lot of powerful people in a lot of trouble. Wyatt and your grandmother continued her work when she had to leave. We have a case if Althea is willing to testify. We need you to bring her home."

Twenty-Two

We have a new executive chef at Vista Mar. Señora Chela's been testing things out in the mornings with her new sous chef, Maria.

Turkey legs with a rich mole that takes hours to construct.

Shredded cabbage, lime, and cilantro, so simple but more delicious than it has any right to be.

Crispy dorado tacos with chipotle pineapple salsa and a bright orange-avocado puree.

Bouillabaisse spiked with chiles and thyme. And I'm sure that's just the beginning.

Shen is back. Wyatt promoted me to front-of-house manager, and Mo's temporarily taken over Rita's host duties. But I can feel her getting restless—the urge to wander will soon have her moving on. I plan to interview prospective hosts as soon as I return. I also know that Mo will eventually circle back to us. That's how it is with the moon.

My midmorning flight, the one I'm taking to find Althea, isn't crowded. She vanished so thoroughly from her life in LA, we can't be sure she's even still living. All I have is the document from the safe deposit box with details of the identity she assumed, and Wyatt's original contacts in Europe where she, to the best of our knowledge, must have made a new life for herself.

Los Angeles and the surrounding counties from the air are a wonder, stretching in a cloudless azure sky, palm tree pseudo-urban monotony of freeways and squat tile-roofed bungalows. As if endless bungalows must have been someone's idea of utopia. Which I suppose, in a way, it is. Old Henry Huntington, the railroad magnate turned real estate tycoon who married his uncle's widow then left behind a very grand estate in San Marino, made a bundle of cash by lobbying for sprawl, the single-family home, and the demise of accessible widespread public transportation. Gran once told me there used to be a network of red and yellow streetcars that could get you just about anywhere in the city—but no more. Instead, the construction of freeways displaced and isolated communities of color, transforming regions over the space of a few years from thriving neighborhoods to what city planners in the forties probably referred to in legal documents as slums.

From above, the city is patches of gray and green with blue swimming pools. Parking lots, brick and concrete hemmed in by endless lines of traffic contrasting with leafy tree-lined streets. The mountains to the north and hills to the south funnel the plane out toward sparse desert but not before one's mind ceases to be able to comprehend the sheer number of people living in this city. This wild place. This wild, cultivated place. Overwhelmed, I lean my forehead against the window. My exhale fogs the heavy plastic, temporarily abstracting the landscape to a blur of melting colors. I become aware of the blood of all who have come before me, the plants and birds and beings who make their home in this city. Though I am on an airplane, thousands of feet above sea level, I can smell the ocean. I breathe into it, touching the quality of the breezes where they meet the tides frothing into the white tops of waves, of dew sinking into thirsty leaves and Pacific mists mixing with the city smog.

My story stretches back into my parents' lives, my grandparents', and so on. We can't know every aspect of the stories we're living out, don't know what happened in the intimate lives of our ancestors. Yet sometimes things happen that crack open the past. Gran's death was like that. Not only did it open my eyes to how I was not living my best life, it also revealed hidden aspects of Gran's life to me—things she chose to hide for good reason. I'd trade all I've learned and gained since then to have her back. But also, I know she's with me.

I love mysteries, how satisfying it is to see everything tied up neatly at the end, puzzle pieces fitting together to form a cohesive whole. Real life isn't like that. In real life, you get a slightly different version from every witness. Pieces are always missing. Early on, I learned to protect myself from disappointment by refusing to move forward. Until I had no choice, I made every effort to remain stuck. It's easier to run up a hill in the dark than in the light. Is it because you can't see how far it is or where you'll end up? Or simply that everything that is not immediate falls away and there is only the movement of breath and blood, the urgency of not falling prey to that darkness behind you.

Settling back into my cramped coach seat, I put on noise-canceling headphones and open my laptop. The flight attendant in the center aisle a few rows ahead shoots me a dirty look. She's in the midst of describing the proper use of a flotation vest should the plane go down over water, so can't come right over to reprimand me. I look away, pretending not to have noticed her disapproval, but then I glance back, because she is somehow familiar. Long bangs curtain her face, concealing much of her features. Her slightly accented voice, delivering the familiar in-case-of-emergency spiel, is unfamiliar. Her slim hands, wrists encased in the blue and gold-braid uniform of the airline, flit through the air, folding the vest, placing it in an overhead compartment, retrieving a pen and notepad from her breast pocket. She scribbles something with a flourish. It's the day of my interview at Vista Mar and I am meeting Rita for the first time. She crosses something out on a list and tells me Wyatt is expecting me. The flight attendant minces down the aisle in her heels toward me, tosses her head, and I can see her face. It is not Rita. I let out the breath I have been holding. Palms sweating, now from relief instead of fear, I reach for the paper she passes over the top of the person seated on the aisle next to me.

It is my name, Queenie Rivers, struck through with a bold, black line.

The flight attendant winks behind her hair, and it *is* Rita, with a different face but the same cunning greenish-yellow irises radiating black lines and mischief. With a jolt, I go to stand, but am jerked back by my seatbelt. Grappling to free myself from the buckle, I lose sight of her for a few crucial seconds before I push past my poor fellow travelers and stumble into the aisle. But where could she go? We're in a plane, thousands of feet in the air. Finding her is not the issue. I'm in such a rush to go after her I slam my head into the overhead compartment—and wake to the pilot announcing that we've reached cruising altitude and we may now use our electronic devices, and a picture book in my lap that the toddler occupying the seat behind me has apparently whacked me over the head with. Her parents apologize profusely and ask if they can buy me a drink to make up for it. My heartrate slowly returns to normal. The flight attendants are a short, curly-haired woman and a man with deep brown skin, bleached hair, and an earring.

Dreams, indeed.

My computer, still shut tight in my lap, has on it a translation of Gran's last journal entry, originally written in a mix of English, Romani, and German, which I sent several weeks ago to the Holocaust studies department at a German university. It arrived in my inbox as I was packing for the trip, and I downloaded it to read on the plane where I could give it my full attention. I retrieve a bottle of water from my backpack and pinch the tender inside of my wrist to make sure I really am awake. It smarts, and I'm reassured, though the eerie feeling of being watched lingers. I pull my headphones out of the pack as well and try to tune out the toddler who is now rhythmically kicking the back of my seat. The document is open on the desktop. I had thought the university might benefit from some of Gran's records, but what she's written is so personal in nature, I almost regret having sent it blindly off to strangers. But then I read it over again and reconsider: these are precisely the types of stories that are missing from the historical record. And I vow to send the university more of Gran's journal entries when I return home.

I worry I am too broken to be a mother and a wife. If I were a man, would I have more options? One thing is certain—if I were a man, I would not be with child. I would likely be as dead as my father and brothers and uncles and cousins, but I would be free. Before I met Wyatt Jones, I considered ending my own life. My family is all dead, why not join them? was my thinking. I survived the camp only to come to America and have my body treated as quarry. Women are commodities here. Beauty is exploited. Lack of it deems a woman worthless.

I do not want to be ungrateful for what Cedric Rivers offers: love, a child, a roof over my head, enough food. But I'm afraid. When one loses so much it's hard to trust life can be good. I don't know if I'll ever feel safe in the world, no matter how safe my corner of the world appears. How will I love Cedric and care for a child when I still dream of my lost sisters every night? A badger is left where it dies in the burrow and the other badgers adjust their tunnels around it. The one that has passed on becomes a part of the architecture, turning, in time, to dust and memory. There is beauty in this example of how the dead adjust the pattern of the livings' tread. It gives me hope. Maybe I don't have to come to terms with the past to embrace life now. Maybe I can lock the past away and . . . simply walk around it until I'm ready to face it. I have tried to make peace with my past, with the assault, but the nightmares always return. Terror is ingrained in my being. I am not ready to relinquish the tunnels I traverse around the dead in exchange for what is known in America as happiness, which Cedric claims is possible. Still, he claims it is possible, even after all he knows, all I've confessed to him, all that has happened. From whence does he get such faith in the future? In people? I don't know if I believe it . . . but I must try. I no longer have only myself to consider.

Gran, a survivor, chose to keep trying, to believe in life . . . for us. For Althea and Randy and Grandad and me. She experienced joy, took pleasure in her daily life. She loved and was loved.

Was she happy?

I want to believe that she was able to heal in her way, despite enduring the toughest of circumstances and then finding herself at the mercy of the American Dream, which, perhaps, does not exist except as a distracting idea meant to call attention away from the darker aspects of collective experience. The notion of "happiness" as prosperity and safety seems, in the context of a story like Gran's, nothing but a farce. Maybe what we as a society are taught to want—the "promise" of our eventual arrival in a state of comfort and ease so long as we pull ourselves up by our bootstraps or whatever—is even a dangerous illusion. Because if we never make it, we feel, deep down, that we have failed. Maybe true happiness is something harder, more complicated, requiring constant labor, attention, risk, and if we are fortunate, growth. A measure of peace, which I do think Gran found.

I click out of email and open the document I began writing during that dark time spent hiding out at Arlo's apartment. I'm still trying to integrate the idea that I have inherited Gran's talent for working beyond the veil of material reality. Though I'm cautious about developing these new skills, what are dreams and visions but the sideways cousins of stories? Gran was an artist, a creator, her life itself a work of art. A story waiting to be written. And that is where I begin.

The sky to the west over Flower Street turns pink as the late-day sun settles low. Anke Weiss shuffles the tarot deck she hand-painted herself by candlelight in the makeshift shelter of blankets and canvas tarpaulins on the bluffs which she currently calls home. She takes her time as she was taught by her mother and aunties years ago in what feels now like another life, before the Nazis came, before those women were all lost.

Clients tend to respect gravity.

If you hurry or push, they think you're hustling. Sometimes you are, sometimes not. One can't always depend on the fates to speak. But one can depend on an empty stomach to protest, and food requires money.

Fortune telling, like anything else, is neither "real" nor "imagined," but both. She knows from experience that no matter how broken a heart may be, there is always choice. That is the gift she gives the people who come to her in search of fortunes. She tells them, as best she can, whatever they need to hear to keep going.

ACKNOWLEDGMENTS

Much gratitude to all who lent their valuable time & attention to this project in a variety of styles & ways: Ellen Meeropol & the wonderful Red Hen Press team, Martha Wydysh, Patricio Cicerone, Elisa Gaffney, Annelise Parham, Mark Valley, Carolyne Topdjian, Karen Winn, Bette Renaud, Stephanie Ripps, Tim Cummings, Lily Brooks-Dalton, Gayle Brandeis, Willie & Holly G.

As a person of (complex) Indigenous descent (New Mexico, Colorado & Mexico), my goal is to offer the Native cultural & mythological elements in this novel as an acknowledgment & recentering of local land-stories, but also an act of borrowing & adapting from cultures that are not my own. Same goes for my representations of all of the diverse cultures & peoples who were, are, and will be intrinsic, essential dwellers in this ancient, sprawling metropolis. In the spirit of myth making & fictional storytelling traditions that hopefully contain kernels of truth, honoring Native & transplanted peoples who call Los Angeles/Tovaangar home, past, present, emerging, thank you.

It seems appropriate to also include the official County of Los Angeles Land Acknowledgment:

The County of Los Angeles recognizes that we occupy land originally and still inhabited and cared for by the Tongva, Tataviam, Serrano, Kizh, and Chumash Peoples. We honor and pay respect to their elders and descendants—past, present, and emerging—as they continue their stewardship of these lands and waters. We acknowledge that settler colonization resulted in land seizure, disease, subjugation, slavery, relocation, broken promises, genocide, and multigenerational trauma. This acknowledgment demonstrates our responsibility and commitment to truth, healing, and reconciliation and to elevating the stories, culture, and community of the original inhabitants of Los Angeles County. We are grateful to have the opportunity to live and work on these ancestral lands. We are dedicated to growing and sustaining relationships with Native peoples and local tribal governments, including (in no particular order) the: Fernandeño Tataviam Band of Mission Indians, Gabrielino Tongva Indians of California Tribal Council, Gabrieleno/Tongva San Gabriel Band of Mission Indians, Gabrieleño Band of Mission Indians—Kizh Nation, San Manuel Band of Mission Indians, San Fernando Band of Mission Indians.

BIOGRAPHICAL NOTE

Malia Márquez was born in New Mexico and grew up in New England. She holds a BFA in 3D Fine Arts from Massachusetts College of Art & Design and an MFA in Creative Writing from Antioch University Los Angeles. Her work in translation has appeared in *Poetry* magazine and her short fiction and essays have been included in various journals and anthologies. She lives with her family in Los Angeles, where she teaches, writes, and wanders around in nature.